TIDAL TREASURES

MAGNOLIA KEY
BOOK FOUR

KAY CORRELL

ZURA LU PUBLISHING LLC

This book is dedicated to my Henry, our new cavalier puppy. You've brought so much laughter and joy to our lives.

ABOUT THIS BOOK

A woman desperate for a fresh start. A chance discovery. And a journey that could change everything.

When Jenna buys an old cottage on Magnolia Key, she's hoping to leave her troubled past behind. But as she peels away layers of wallpaper, she uncovers more than just dated decor—she finds a hidden box containing love letters from the 1920s.

Drawn into the mystery of star-crossed lovers from long ago, Jenna finds herself falling for Nash, the charming local contractor helping her renovate. But as she digs deeper into the island's secrets, she realizes that some mysteries are better left unsolved.

In this heartwarming tale of second

chances and small-town charm, Jenna must decide if she's ready to confront the ghosts of her past and open her heart to a future filled with love and belonging.

Welcome to Magnolia Key, where old secrets and new beginnings intertwine like sea grass in the coastal breeze

KAY'S BOOKS

Find more information on all my books at
kaycorrell.com
Buy direct from Kay's Shop at
shop.kaycorrell.com

COMFORT CROSSING ~ THE SERIES

The Wedding in the Grove - (a crossover short story between series - with Josephine and Paul from The Letter.)

LIGHTHOUSE POINT ~ THE SERIES
Wish Upon a Shell - Book One
Wedding on the Beach - Book Two
Love at the Lighthouse - Book Three
Cottage near the Point - Book Four
Return to the Island - Book Five
Bungalow by the Bay - Book Six
Christmas Comes to Lighthouse Point - Book Seven

CHARMING INN ~ Return to Lighthouse Point
One Simple Wish - Book One
Two of a Kind - Book Two
Three Little Things - Book Three
Four Short Weeks - Book Four
Five Years or So - Book Five
Six Hours Away - Book Six
Charming Christmas - Book Seven

SWEET RIVER ~ THE SERIES
A Dream to Believe in - Book One
A Memory to Cherish - Book Two

A Song to Remember - Book Three
A Time to Forgive - Book Four
A Summer of Secrets - Book Five
A Moment in the Moonlight - Book Six

MOONBEAM BAY ~ THE SERIES

The Parker Women - Book One
The Parker Cafe - Book Two
A Heather Parker Original - Book Three
The Parker Family Secret - Book Four
Grace Parker's Peach Pie - Book Five
The Perks of Being a Parker - Book Six

BLUE HERON COTTAGES ~ THE SERIES

Memories of the Beach - Book One
Walks along the Shore - Book Two
Bookshop near the Coast - Book Three
Restaurant on the Wharf - Book Four
Lilacs by the Sea - Book Five
Flower Shop on Magnolia - Book Six
Christmas by the Bay - Book Seven
Sea Glass from the Past - Book Eight

MAGNOLIA KEY ~ THE SERIES

Saltwater Sunrise - Book One
Encore Echoes - Book Two

Coastal Candlelight - Book Three
Tidal Treasures - Book Four
And more to come!

CHRISTMAS SEASHELLS AND SNOWFLAKES
Seaside Christmas Wishes

WIND CHIME BEACH ~ A stand-alone novel

INDIGO BAY ~
Sweet Days by the Bay - Kay's Complete Collection of stories in the Indigo Bay series

Sign up for my newsletter at my website *kaycorrell.com* to make sure you don't miss any new releases or sales.

CHAPTER 1

Jenna pulled her car to a stop in front of the weathered cottage, its faded blue shutters and peeling paint a clear picture of its age and neglect. She turned off the engine and sat for a moment, still gripping the steering wheel of her old, sensible sedan as she took in the sight of her new home.

Well, the cottage certainly wasn't new, but it was her home now. The salty breeze from the ocean ruffled her hair, carrying with it the distant cries of seagulls and the gentle lapping of waves against the shore. This is what she wanted. Peace. Quiet. Solitude.

She stepped out of the car, her feet crunching on the crushed shell driveway. The cottage looked smaller than she remembered from the listing photos, but there was a certain charm to its quaint appearance. She couldn't believe she'd bought the house sight unseen, including the contents. But her Realtor had done a walkthrough and sent her videos of it. She'd fallen in love with it as soon as she saw the view out the big picture windows. The cottage looked smaller than she remembered from the listing photos, but the surrounding greenery was even more lush in person. She was certain there was potential hidden beneath the cottage's worn exterior. The porch sagged slightly, and the white paint was peeling in places, but there was a certain charm to it all—a sense of history and character that drew her in.

Jenna walked up the creaky wooden steps to the front porch, fishing the keys out of her pocket. The door stuck slightly as she turned the key in the lock, but with a firm pull, it swung open, revealing a musty interior. She stepped inside, her footsteps echoing on the worn wood floors. She coughed as specks of dust danced in the sunlight streaming through the windows, illuminating the sparse furnishings left behind by the previous owner.

The floorboards creaked in protest as she crossed over to the windows, running her finger along the sill, feeling the grit of years of neglect. Faded floral wallpaper clung to the walls, and a clock on the far wall was permanently stuck at three thirty-two.

She wandered into the kitchen, where dated appliances greeted her. But the inspector had assured her they were all in working order. She opened to cabinets to find a few random pots and pans and dishes. The cabinets needed a good scrubbing before she filled them with the cooking items she'd brought with her.

She went back into the living room and over to the built-in bookcase. There, on a high shelf, a tarnished silver picture frame beckoned her. She gently picked it up and brushed away the dust with the side of her hand to reveal a faded black-and-white photograph. A smiling couple stood in front of the cottage. The woman's hair was styled in soft waves and the man had his arm around her waist. Their faces radiated contentment and joy.

And maybe that peace she was so longing for herself.

She studied the photograph, wondering about the couple's life here in the cottage. Had they been happy? Had they lived out their dreams? She felt a sudden kinship with the couple, a connection that spanned the decades between them. And at the same time a wistfulness settled over her, a yearning for all that was missing in her life.

She placed the photograph carefully on the shelf and continued exploring the cottage. A mix of excitement and uncertainty flooded through her. This was a fresh start, a chance to leave behind painful memories and disappointments.

She had always dreamed of living in a small coastal town, far from the hustle and bustle of the city and the demands of her high-pressure job as an investigative reporter. And she couldn't believe her good luck when she'd found this cottage for sale on Magnolia Key. The very island she'd vacationed on as a young girl, coming back for a month's stay each summer. Eventually, when she and her sister had gotten older and had been involved in so many activities with school and sports, the trips stopped. But she'd never forgotten the island.

Now that she was here, standing in the middle of her new home, the reality of her decision began to sink in. She was alone, in an unfamiliar place, with no friends or family nearby. The cottage needed work, more than she had initially anticipated, and she wondered if she had taken on more than she could handle. But then, she didn't mind hard work. It would keep her busy. Keep her mind off why she was really here...

Shaking away her thoughts, she moved through the cottage, carefully checking out each room. She'd seen photos and the video, but neither had done justice to how charming this cottage was. Or would be after she fixed it up. She went into the main bedroom and crossed over to the large bay window. There, the gulf stretched out before her, the sunlight sparkling like diamonds on the waves.

When she returned to the living room, she yanked off the sheets covering the furniture, sending a cloud of dust billowing into the room. The faded floral couch was still in good shape, if not really her style. Maybe she could make slipcovers for it. She laughed out loud. To do that, she'd have to learn to sew first and buy a sewing machine. Shaking her head at her silliness, she crossed over to the large windows flanking the back of the house. She threw them open, letting the fresh sea air rush in and chase away the damp, dusty smell. She sucked in a deep breath, savoring the tangy sea air.

Flashes of the life she left behind flickered into her thoughts. The endless hours as an investigative reporter, a job that had consumed her life. Always digging. Always chasing stories. Any relationship she'd tried to have crumbled under her dedication to her job and the long hours. And look where that had led her. Here, to her escape to Magnolia Key.

Jenna put down the broom as her phone rang. She glanced at the screen. Marly. Her sister checking on her, no doubt.

"Hey, sis. Yes, I made it to Magnolia just fine."

"I still can't believe you just up and moved all the way across the country. You... you didn't need to do that."

"I did. I needed a change. I needed to get away. I'm done with the whole investigative reporter thing. I... I can't do it anymore."

"It wasn't your fault," Marly insisted.

"And yet, it was. My actions had consequences." How many times did she have to have this same conversation with Marly?

"You're too hard on yourself."

"Can we just skip it? Let's not get into it again." She grabbed some cleaning supplies out of a box as if that would make Marly stop this line of questioning.

"Okay, but you know you can move back at any time. You could live with me until you found a new place to stay."

"I'm not moving back. Made a killing on my house when I sold it. Enough for a large down payment on this one."

"How is it now that you've had a chance to see it in person?"

"It's lovely." Well, it would be after she finished working on it.

"Is it?" Her sister sounded skeptical. "I saw the photos."

"It will be fine once I do some repairs. And they'll keep me busy."

Marly sighed. "I could come and help."

"No, I just need time. I'm looking forward to this."

"You did take that rundown house here in San Francisco that no one would have believed could be saved and turned it into a charming home."

"I'll do the same to this one." She glanced around the room. With a lot of work…

"Okay, but I'm going to call and check on you. Often."

"Of course you will." Knowing her sister, the calls would be daily.

"I miss you."

"Miss you too. You can come visit me after I get the cottage all fixed up."

She clicked off her phone and looked at her watch. It was only late morning. She could do this. She'd tackle this mess right away.

All afternoon, Jenna threw herself into cleaning the cottage, scrubbing every surface, washing blinds, cleaning windows. By evening she'd made a dent in the grime and dust and unpacked the boxes she'd hauled with her. There were a few items she'd shipped that should arrive sometime this week, but she hadn't wanted to bring a lot with her. She'd wanted to leave her past behind.

She stood with her hands on her hips, surveying her accomplishments. But there was still so much to do. Two of the cabinet doors had fallen off when she opened them to clean the shelves. A couple of windows wouldn't open and several were missing screens. The front porch steps were definitely a hazard to anyone coming here, so they would need fixing. She wanted to strip the floral wallpaper and paint the walls a soft, pale, buttercream color. The lights in the main bedroom flickered, so she needed to get an electrician out to check the wiring. The refrigerator worked… but just barely. She'd probably have to replace that.

Then there was the outside. It desperately needed a good coat of paint. She didn't mind doing the lower section, but she wasn't much on climbing ladders to paint the upper portion.

She went to the kitchen and sat at the table, writing a to-do list of repairs. As she pushed back from the table, she dropped her pen on the pad of paper. It was official. She was in over her head and was going to have to find some help.

She walked to the counter and poked around in the box of food she'd brought, seeing there wasn't much to fix for supper. She sliced an apple and made a plate of cheese and crackers. After pouring a glass of wine, she headed out to the deck overlooking the ocean. Grateful for the one rocking chair the previous owner had left, she sank onto it and set her glass on the table beside it. She rocked gently in the chair as the sun made its slow descent to the horizon and the sky burst into brilliant colors.

Time seemed to slow as the darkness crept

in. Her gaze drifted to the far horizon where the inky black of the night sky met the dark expanse of the ocean. Stars blinked above her as she searched the sky for familiar constellations. Nothing she could have seen in the city back home in San Francisco.

No, that wasn't home. *This* was home now.

Tomorrow she'd explore the town and see what had changed and what had remained the same. Hope sprang inside her that she could make this house feel like a home and finally find some peace.

CHAPTER 2

B everly heard the familiar jingle of the cafe's front door opening and glanced up from wiping down the counter, greeting the first customer of the day with a warm smile.

"Good morning, Nash." She reached for a clean mug and poured his usual dark roast. The rich aroma of freshly brewed coffee filled the air, mingling with the comforting scents of baked goods and the faint tang of the ocean breeze wafting in from outside. "Right on time as always."

Nash nodded in greeting, his weathered features softening as he returned her smile. He leaned against the counter, engaging in their daily ritual of friendly banter. "You know me,

Bev. Creature of habit. Wouldn't want to throw off your whole morning routine."

"I appreciate that," she teased as she slid the steaming mug across the worn wooden surface, its edges smoothed by years of use and care. "Here you go, one black coffee for my most reliable customer."

"Don't let your other customers hear you playing favorites," he said with a wink as he accepted the mug. The corners of his eyes crinkled, and a hint of mischief danced in his gaze.

Nash had been a fixture at Coastal Coffee for as long as Beverly could remember, their morning coffee routine an ingrained part of their lives. He was her first customer of the day almost every single day. He took his mug, moved over to a table, and sat down, taking a sip of his coffee as the sleepy town began to stir around them.

Beverly's gaze drifted to the entrance as the door swung open, signaling the arrival of a new customer. An unfamiliar woman hesitated before stepping inside. The woman had a pensive expression, her eyes scanning the cozy interior of the shop.

As the newcomer approached the counter,

Beverly greeted her. "Good morning. What can I get for you?"

"I'm hoping for breakfast and coffee." She smiled sheepishly. "Really, really need the coffee."

Beverly's laugh mingled with the woman's, establishing an instant camaraderie. "I know how it is. Can't really get my day started without it. Go ahead and make yourself comfortable. Grab a table and take a seat anywhere and I'll bring you a cup."

The woman nodded gratefully and began to head toward a secluded table near the back, but Beverly stopped her with a playful shake of her head. "Ah, not that one, hon. That's Miss Eleanor's usual spot. She'll be in soon. And we've all learned to keep Miss Eleanor happy." She winked conspiratorially.

The newcomer settled into a cozy corner table, continuing to survey the surroundings as if trying to absorb every detail.

Beverly brought her coffee. "Specials up on the board." She nodded to the chalkboard over the counter. "Cinnamon rolls today. They're delicious. Get them from the mainland fresh each day. I'm Beverly, by the way. Owner and chief coffee wrangler."

"I'm Jenna. I just bought a place here on Magnolia Key. Moved in yesterday."

"Ah, a newcomer to our little slice of paradise. You didn't happen to buy the old Weston place, did you?"

"I did. How did you know?"

Beverly chuckled. "Small town. Word travels faster than storm winds here. I'm glad someone finally scooped it up. It's been sitting empty for years while the family squabbled over what to do with it. Guess there was some kind of argument going on between the kids after their parents passed away. Some wanted to sell, some wanted to keep it." Beverly shrugged. "Not always easy when parents die and there's an estate to be settled and the heirs have differing opinions. The cottage has been neglected for years. Will be nice to see it all fixed up."

"I have to admit, I'm in a bit over my head. It definitely needs more work than I anticipated." Jenna gave a self-deprecating laugh. "I don't mind hard work, but some of it is out of the depths of skill and my knowledge."

"You're in luck then. Nash over there"—she gestured toward his table near the front window — "he's the best contractor this side of the

Mississippi. If anyone can whip that old place into shape, it's him."

A thoughtful expression settled over Jenna's features as she looked over at him. "You know, that's probably not a bad idea to at least talk to him about it."

"Nash," Beverly called out, beckoning him over with a wave. "Pop over here for a second and meet our newest neighbor. This is Jenna— she's the one who bought the Weston cottage."

Pushing back his chair, Nash rose and ambled toward them, a friendly smile crinkling the corners of his eyes. "Ma'am," he greeted Jenna with a polite nod.

Jenna tilted her head up slightly, meeting the piercing gaze of the most striking pair of sky-blue eyes she'd ever seen. The man—Nash— reached out a calloused hand in greeting, his grip firm and confident as she accepted the handshake. His large hand enveloped hers.

"Oh, call me Jenna, please."

"Yes, ma'am." He gave her a small smile. "Jenna, I mean." His voice was a rich, unhurried baritone.

"Jenna's looking at getting some help with repairing the old Weston place," Beverly chimed in.

"Ah, yes. It needs some work, doesn't it? It's a real shame the family let it fall into such disrepair over the years."

"It does need quite a bit of attention. I plan to tackle a lot of it myself. But some of it, like the electricity and the outside painting, are beyond my skill set. Plus, I hate high ladders."

Nash grinned. "Yep, those high ladders can be a bit troublesome, can't they? How about I drop by this afternoon and take a look at things? That work for you?"

"It does, thank you."

Nash nodded again and returned to his table. He slipped into his chair with an easy grace and confidence, as if he belonged there. A regular. She suddenly felt out of place, a blatant outsider.

Beverly nodded toward Nash. "He's a good craftsman. I'm sure you'll be pleased with any work he or his crew does."

"Thank you for hooking me up with Nash. I mean... not hooking up. Not like dating hookups. I mean..." The warmth of a blush flushed her cheeks. "For suggesting that he help with the repairs."

"Glad to help." Beverly nodded.

"I used to come here to Magnolia Key as a girl, but it is a bit strange moving to a totally new place. I saw lots had changed on my walk over here this morning. And yet, I was happy to see much has stayed the same."

"We're not really big on change." Beverly laughed. "And that explains why you moved here. Magnolia Key has a way of pulling people back once they've come here."

Jenna offered a small smile, hoping to deflect any probing questions about her motivations for relocating to Magnolia Key. "I'm hoping for a bit of a slower pace," she explained simply. "I'm from San Francisco and I was… tired of it." And exhausted and disheartened with her job, but Beverly didn't need to know those details. And Jenna didn't want to think about it. Not anymore.

"Ah, a big city woman. Well, I'm sure you'll find that slower pace here on Magnolia." Beverly smiled and with a nod, she shifted topics. "Now, have you decided what you want for breakfast? You look like you could use a nice hot meal."

"I'll have two eggs scrambled, hash browns... and I'll probably regret this, but I'll have a cinnamon roll too."

"Great choice." Beverly grinned with approval as she headed toward the kitchen. "I'll have your food out in a jiffy."

Jenna sat waiting for her food and sipping the delicious coffee. She really needed to make a run to the market and stock up on essentials. Coffee for sure, and a bit of everything. She wanted to fully stock her pantry. She loved to cook, and now she would have the time to indulge in it. No more grabbing something on the way home from work. But for now, she just basked in the cozy atmosphere of the coffee shop.

An older woman came in and strode across the floor with a no-nonsense attitude. She claimed the table Beverly had dubbed Miss Eleanor's. Beverly came out immediately with a pitcher of cream and a mug of coffee, setting them before the woman with a practiced ease that hinted at their well-established routine. Miss Eleanor's demeanor exuded an air of belonging. Here at Coastal Coffee, at her table, on Magnolia Key.

Jenna wondered if she'd ever feel like she really belonged here. Hopefully, in time, she would.

CHAPTER 3

J enna peered out the window, her breath catching slightly as the rumble of a truck pulling up the driveway reached her ears. She took in the details of his older vehicle, a well-used pickup in a sapphire blue color. Carlisle Construction was emblazoned on the truck doors.

The driver's side door opened and Nash stepped out, his broad shoulders filling out his well-worn t-shirt. Jenna's gaze lingered perhaps a moment too long before she blinked and pulled herself together. She smoothed her hands down the front of her t-shirt, noticing a streak of dirt along the hem from her attempts at cleaning the windows. She made her way to the front door and opened it. Her breath caught slightly as Nash's warm smile crinkled the corners of his eyes just like it had this morning.

"Afternoon, ma'am… Jenna." His rich voice washed over her. "Let's see what kind of work we have in store."

She stepped back, allowing him to enter, and the scent of freshly cut wood and fresh ocean air wafted in with him. His tanned, muscular arm grazed her own as he brushed past.

Jenna watched Nash's eyes scan the space, taking in the dated decor and the areas in need of repair. She felt a pang of self-consciousness, but his expression remained neutral. He glanced into the kitchen and turned back to her.

"Well, this place has good bones," he commented, his gaze lingering on the exposed beams overhead. "Solid construction. They don't build them like this anymore."

Jenna nodded, feeling a flicker of pride in her new home despite its current state. "It's about one hundred years old, though there have been some renovations and updates. Not sure what else. I fell in love with the character of it. The history."

Nash turned to her, his blue eyes crinkling at the corners. "I can see why. It's got a lot of potential." He gestured to the living room. "We could open up this space, maybe knock out that wall to let in more light. And the kitchen could use some updating, but we can work with the layout."

"I don't mind the kitchen. I kind of like it. Love the old stove and the big sink. But I do like the idea of taking out that wall between this main room and the kitchen. Make it all one large great room. That works for me. And that should lighten both spaces."

"Okay, we'll keep the kitchen as is." He jotted a note on a small notepad, then carefully poked around the cottage and went out to the deck, nodding occasionally as he made his notes. Nash was a nodder, that was for sure. She followed him from room to room.

"Afraid some of the plumbing needs some work. And some of the electrical. Want to check out your roof, too."

"The inspector who checked out the house before I bought it said the roof was about ten years old."

"Ah, probably had to replace when that hurricane came through here about then."

As Nash continued to share his insights and suggestions, Jenna found herself relaxing, drawn in by his enthusiasm and expertise. He seemed to see beyond the peeling paint and worn floors to the heart of the cottage, to what it could become. As they continued the tour, discussing ideas for the renovation, Jenna was surprised by how at ease she felt in his presence. He had a calming energy about him, a steadiness that put her nerves to rest.

"I think the first step is to address any structural issues," he said as he flipped through his notes. "Then we can move on to the cosmetic stuff."

She nodded, wondering about the cost of such repairs. She knew the renovation would be a significant investment—more than she'd planned on—but she was determined to see it through.

They returned to the main room. Nash turned to her. "So, what made you decide to buy this place? It does need some work, but the view is spectacular."

"I, um, I needed a fresh start," Jenna admitted. "I had to… get away from my old life. Start again. I'd come to the island as a young girl, and this place just… called to me, you know?"

Nash's eyes softened, his expression one of understanding. "Everyone's got a past, Jenna," he said gently, holding her gaze. There was not a hint of judgment in his tone, only a gentle reassurance. "What matters is what you do from here on out."

Something inside of her unclenched at his words, a tightness she hadn't even known she was carrying. "I hope you're right. I'm hoping this place will help me... find some peace."

The words hung in the air between them, more candid than she'd intended. But there was something about Nash that put her at ease, an innate trustworthiness that she couldn't quite put her finger on.

He nodded yet again, his expression open and compassionate. "We all need a little peace sometimes," he said simply. "This town, this island... it has a way of providing that if you let it."

She relaxed even more at his words and encouragement. She could almost imagine what it would be like to let the gentle rhythm of island life soothe her. "I hope so." Her gaze drifted back to him. There was a steadiness about him, a strength she felt herself drawn to. A solidness in the midst of her own personal storm.

She pulled her gaze from him and cleared

her throat. "I appreciate you taking the time to come out here. I know I'm new in town, and you must be busy with other projects."

Nash waved off her concern with a smile. "Happy to help. We take care of our own here on the island. And now you're one of us." He paused, his expression turning more serious. "I know it can be tough, starting over in a new place. But you'll find folks here are quick to lend a hand."

A rush of gratitude flowed through her at his words and the kindness in his eyes. Maybe moving to Magnolia Key wasn't such a crazy idea after all. She walked him to the door and watched as he climbed back into his truck. With a wave, he pulled out of the drive. Maybe, just maybe, she'd found more than a new home in Magnolia Key. Maybe she'd found a place to belong.

Nash pulled away from Jenna's cottage, the truck tires crunching on the shell driveway. He glanced in the rearview mirror and could already envision the transformation that a few fresh coats of paint would bring to the weathered structure, turning it into a warm and inviting home.

This woman intrigued him. She had appeared out of nowhere and purchased the old Weston place—now that the heirs had quit their squabbling and agreed to sell it before it crumbled into a place unable to be made habitable. He had to admit it had chafed him to drive by the cottage for all these years and see how the family had neglected it, allowing its once charming appearance to fall into disrepair. But now it looked like the cottage was getting a new chance. It would have someone living in it who appreciated it.

He smiled at his thoughts, knowing it was a bit strange to believe that buildings had feelings and a unique character, but to him, they did. Just a result of growing up and learning the construction trade from his father. His dad always said that each home has a heart of its own.

He sighed as he rolled to a stop at the one intersection in town with stop signs. Not that it really needed it. Never enough traffic to justify it. But a mayor a few years back had insisted Magnolia needed them. But the stop sign still annoyed him.

He continued on to his house but couldn't get thoughts of Jenna out of his mind. It was a bit odd that she'd just up and moved to the island though. Most folks around Magnolia Key had roots going back generations with their histories intertwined like the branches on the old live oak tree in the town square. He remembered the stories his grandfather would tell about the island's founding families, their struggles and triumphs, all woven into the very fabric of the town.

It was rare for a total stranger to come to the island and settle down. But then, Tori Duran had moved here a while back and reopened the theater—but she'd been to the island often with her grandmother when she was a girl, and that's what made her choose to come live here. Although Jenna had said the same thing. She'd come here as a child. Seemed like Magnolia Key did have a way of calling people back.

Well, he'd never even left the island. Lived here his whole life. Took over the construction company from his father, who had taken it over from his grandfather. Three generations of Carlisle Construction.

Unbidden, his thoughts popped right back to Jenna. He couldn't quite figure her out. She said she wanted to do as much work as she could herself. He got that. Repairs could get expensive. But she looked at the cottage with a gaze that said she knew it could be turned into something wonderful.

Still, there had been a slightly wistful air about her, maybe even a hint of melancholy, and the distinct feeling she was hiding something or running away from something. She hadn't elaborated on why she'd come here or why she needed peace so desperately.

He felt a protective instinct flare up deep inside. There was something about her that intrigued him. An underlying strength that captivated him. And although he'd just met her, he found himself wanting to find a way to chase away that haunted look from her chestnut-brown eyes. To see her relax, see her laugh.

Her project, her desire to restore the rundown home, spoke to him on a deeper level. Maybe because it was more than just fixing a broken-down cottage. Jenna seemed intent on not only rebuilding the cottage but rebuilding her own life.

And he had the ability to help her with that. Help her shed whatever turmoil she'd left behind to come here to Magnolia Key to start over.

He was crazy busy with construction work right now, but somehow he'd find a way to fit her into the schedule. He vowed to give her the best deal possible on the repairs so she wouldn't have to live in construction chaos for long. And if he personally helped with the repairs? Well, that would just give him a chance to get to know her better.

CHAPTER 4

J enna answered the knock at the door the
next morning, surprised to see Nash
standing there. She blinked from the glare
of the bright morning sun.

"Ma'am." He dipped his head in a nod.

"Jenna," she gently insisted.

"Hard habit to break." He flashed her a
sheepish smile. "Anyway, I realized I didn't get
your phone number, so I couldn't text or call to
let you know I have some estimates ready. Hope
this isn't too early to stop by."

"Not at all. I've been up for hours." She self-
consciously tucked an unruly strand of hair
behind her ear, painfully aware of the slash of
dried paint on her t-shirt. What must he think to
always find her in such disarray?

He stood there on her front step, shifting from foot to foot.

"Oh, come in." She stepped aside, and he walked in. "I was just doing some touch-up painting. Found some left-over kitchen paint and I'm touching up some dings in the wall."

He nodded again and held out some papers. "I could go over these with you. Some things are absolutely necessary for safety reasons, but others are more optional, depending on your needs and your budget." He handed her the bid he'd prepared.

She took the papers, trying to hide her apprehension about what the numbers would reveal. She walked over to the window, scanning down the page. She finally looked up at him. "It's a bit more than I'd planned on," she admitted, biting her lower lip.

"I understand." He crossed over to where she was standing. A scent of freshly cut wood clung to him. "We can trim it down some. Leave that wall for now, if money's tight." His calloused finger traced a line on the bid. "That would hold costs down."

"I did think taking the wall down was a good idea, but budget-wise, it's probably best to leave it."

"I appreciate your honesty about what your budget is. The items on page three are just suggestions. We could see how things go with the necessary work, and then if you want to add on more later, we can. Just check the number at the bottom of page one."

She looked at the number, relieved it was much more in line with what she'd hoped to spend. And maybe she could tackle some of the smaller projects herself. She glanced up at him. "This sounds reasonable. We'll start with the items on the first page."

He nodded. "Sounds good. I could start the beginning of next week if that works for you."

"So soon? That's wonderful. I can't wait to get the place fixed up and make it feel more like home."

"Afraid there'll be the usual construction chaos while the work is being done."

"I'm sure there will be. But I'll just keep in mind the outcome will be worth it."

"If you could pick out the color you want the house painted, and the trim color, that would be great. And just let me know. I'll buy it with my discount. My phone number is on the top of the bid. Text or call anytime if you have any questions."

"I really appreciate this."

"It's no problem, ma'—Jenna." His eyes twinkled as he corrected himself.

She smiled. "I'll see you on Monday, then?"

"I'll be here with some of my crew and we'll get things started. I'll try to make sure the job doesn't run on too long." He gave her a warm smile that reached up to his eyes.

"That would be great." Her heart did a double beat for no reason that she could fathom as she tore her gaze from his bright blue eyes.

She walked him to the door and watched as he swung up into his truck. He waved once, and the engine of his truck rumbled as he pulled out of the drive.

Wouldn't be the worst thing to have him hanging around the cottage for a bit during repairs.

Late that afternoon, Jenna stood in the paint aisle at the hardware store, surrounded by an overwhelming array of colors. She could go with white—a safe choice—but she longed for some color on the house. Many of the cottages that lined the beach were painted in bright colors, but a pale shade suited her better. But which one?

She held up different shades, trying to envision how they might transform the weathered exterior of her new cottage. A soft yellow, perhaps? Or a muted blue to complement the ocean breeze?

"Need some help?"

She turned around at the familiar voice to find Nash standing there with a warm smile on his face.

"I'm having trouble deciding on the perfect color," she admitted, waving the fistful of color cards she held toward the display. "There are so many options."

Nash stepped closer, his broad shoulders brushing against hers as he surveyed the colors. She tried not to focus on the faint woodsy scent that surrounded him or the way his shirt stretched across his muscular back.

Get a grip. She concentrated on the color display.

"Well, you definitely want something that complements the beach setting," he mused, plucking a few swatches from the array. "These cooler tones might work nicely—maybe a pale aqua or soft gray?"

Jenna considered the colors he'd selected, holding them up one by one. The gentle blue-green hue did seem to capture the essence of the ocean. "I like this one," she said, her finger tracing the swatch labeled 'Sea Glass.'

A smile tugged at the corners of Nash's mouth. "Sea Glass it is, then. It will look perfect. And we'll get your home all fixed up."

We. A tiny hint of a thrill went with her. Nash would be with her as she whipped her cottage into shape. Just as quickly, she realized that maybe by "we" Nash meant he and his workers. Not the two of them. Yes, that was probably what he meant. He might even want her to stay out of the way.

She bit her bottom lip, uncertainty teasing her.

Seriously, woman. Get a grip. Since when are you so tentative?

She cleared her throat, still clutching the sea glass color swatch in her hand. "Thank you for your help. I really appreciate it. It felt like such a big decision."

"Picking a house color is a big decision. It brings out the personality of the house." He grinned self-consciously. "Well, I feel like houses have personalities."

The fact that he believed that warmed her heart. She hoped he'd help turn her cottage into a home that felt like hers.

His eyes lingered on her face, then he nodded. "I should be going."

She nodded in return. Was she going to pick up his nodding habit? He turned away, and a void surrounded her, as if a piece of her new life was slipping away. Why was she thinking such foolish thoughts? She shook her head.

Nash stopped at the end of the aisle, turned, and walked a few steps back toward her. "Say, I was just getting ready to head to Sharky's for dinner. The seafood place on the boardwalk. Would you care to join me?"

Surprise flickered through her. She hesitated, unsure if it was wise to spend more time with him given her crazy thoughts. But the thought of eating alone in her cottage held little appeal. "Sure, that sounds nice."

They went outside and walked together down the boardwalk, heading to the restaurant. "I remember going to Sharky's when I came here as a girl. I'm surprised it's still here."

"It sure is. Though the original Sharky is long gone. But we still call whoever runs it Sharky. A town gets set in its ways." He grinned.

Jenna relaxed as they walked along. The early evening sun was softening and splashing rays across the water. A pair of seagulls flew past, calling noisily to each other. It was all so peaceful here. A slower pace. She was pleasantly surprised at how rapidly she was getting used to it.

They entered Sharky's, and she was pleased that not much had changed. The rustic wooden interior and lively atmosphere greeted them. The scent of grilled fish and fried seafood filled the air, making Jenna's stomach rumble. They took a table near the back.

As they perused the menus, Jenna stole a few glances at Nash. His strong jawline was dusted with stubble, and his eyes held a depth that intrigued her. She wondered about his past, about the stories that lay hidden beneath his relaxed exterior. So far, he always seemed calm and collected. She wondered if anything ever ruffled him.

He caught her staring and gave her an easy smile. "Made up your mind?"

She blushed. Was he asking what she thought of him or what she wanted for dinner?

"Lots of great choices on the menu," he added.

Okay, he was talking about the food. "I'm going to have the fried grouper sandwich. I hope it's as good as it used to be."

"Oh, it is. Not much changes here at Sharky's."

The waitress came and took their order, and a silence fell between them. She wanted to ask him questions about his life and get to know him better. She couldn't help it. Her background as an investigative reporter always made her want to ask questions. But she'd left that life behind, she reminded herself.

Nash leaned back in his chair, relaxed, and stretched out his legs. "So, Jenna. Tell me about yourself."

"I… uh… what do you want to know?"

"Where you grew up. Any family? What's your favorite color?" He sent her an impish grin.

She laughed. "Favorite color is yellow. Favorite food is a toss-up between apple pie and pizza." She shrugged. "I know, far apart on the food chain and not healthy, but there you have it."

"Have to admit, it's hard to beat a slice of apple pie."

"I grew up in Wisconsin but ended up in

San Francisco because my sister, Marly, lived there."

"What do you do for a living?"

And there it was. The question she always dreaded now. "I am…" She swallowed. "I *was* an investigative reporter." That career was over. She still freelanced some articles for different news outlets, but nothing that required more than simple research. No digging deep. No uncovering secrets.

"That sounds interesting. But you're not anymore?" He cocked an eyebrow questioningly.

"No, that's behind me now." She wanted to just leave it at that, so she changed the subject. "My sister, Marly, is a bit peeved that I left San Francisco, but she knew I needed a change. She was surprised I ended up here on Magnolia Key, though. But she has fond memories of it too. I'm sure she'll come visit soon."

"That will be nice."

"Probably, but she's a bit bossy and opinionated. I guess older sisters have that right." She smiled.

She figured it was her turn to ask him a few questions. Nothing prying or deep. Nothing like when she was trying to uncover the secrets of someone's life for an investigative piece. Just some friendly banter, right?

"So, how about you? Family? Favorite color?" She smiled at him, turning the tables.

"Lots of family. My parents still live here on the island. Took over the construction business from my dad." Nash laughed. "He still comes to some of the job sites. Guess he's checking up on me. I have two sisters and a brother. They live on the mainland though. And my older sister is bossy, just like yours." He winked.

The waitress came with their meals, interrupting their conversation. Jenna dove into her grouper sandwich with gusto. Nash was right. It was still wonderful. They chatted about the town as they ate their meal. An easy camaraderie that she welcomed. It made her feel a tiny bit less like an outsider to the island. Having a nice meal with a local.

When they finished their meal, Nash insisted on paying for both of them. "No, you don't have to do that," she protested.

"My pleasure. Just a little welcome to the island dinner."

They headed outside as the sun was beginning to slip below the horizon. Brilliant colors lit up the sky. She motioned toward the display. "This is what I remember about Magnolia. The sunsets. They are spectacular."

"I admit, the island does like to show off its sunsets." His lips tipped up in a smile.

"Well, I should head home." She stood on the boardwalk beside him.

"Can I walk you back to your cottage?"

"You don't have to do that. I'll be fine."

"My momma wouldn't forgive me if she found out I didn't walk you home. And she's probably already heard that we just had dinner together." He broke into a wide grin. "My momma keeps pretty close tabs on me even though I'm a grown man. And news travels quickly on the island." He winked.

"I sure wouldn't want you to get in trouble with your mom." She put on a serious expression, smothering a grin.

"You wouldn't." He met her serious expression, but his eyes twinkled.

They slowly walked back to her cottage, and he followed her up the steps to her door. She unlocked the door and turned to him. "Thank you for dinner. It was nice to have company for a meal."

"My pleasure. And I'll see you bright and early Monday morning." He turned and walked away. She stood on the porch and watched until he disappeared down the road before she went inside and flipped on the light.

The mess she'd left greeted her. A bucket of murky cleaning water sat near the bank of windows. The papers with the work that needed to be done and the bid from Nash rested on the coffee table. A smattering of tools sat on the bookshelf. She'd started lightly sanding some nicks on the bookcases to get them ready for a new coat of protective finish. The wood was a wonderful, worn cherry, and they looked to be custom made.

She ran her gaze around the cottage. So much work to be done.

But then, Nash would be here to help her. The thought comforted her and helped keep some of her overwhelm at bay.

CHAPTER 5

The next morning, Jenna headed to Coastal Coffee. She had groceries to make her own breakfast, but she found herself craving some company. She strolled along the sidewalks as the early morning sun warmed her face. A light breeze off the water lifted tendrils of her hair. It was nice to be able to walk to so many places here on the island. Her car had barely moved since she'd been here.

She stepped into the cafe, smiling as the bell over the door jingled its welcome. The cozy atmosphere embraced her, along with the enticing aroma of freshly brewed coffee and baked goods.

Beverly waved to her. "Take a seat. Be with you in a sec."

She took a table, careful not to sit at the one she'd been told was Miss Eleanor's. Beverly came over and plopped a mug on the table. "Coffee?"

"Yes, please." She gazed up at the chalkboard over the counter and her mouth watered. Everything sounded delicious.

"You just missed Nash," Beverly said as she set the coffeepot down on the table.

Jenna arched an eyebrow. "Missed him?"

Beverly chuckled. "I heard you had dinner with him at Sharky's last night."

A blush crept onto her cheeks. "He told you that?"

"Hon, I knew it before your food even hit the table." Beverly laughed, a warm, melodic sound. "News travels faster than a summer storm around here. This is a small island."

Jenna smiled at the woman's candor. "I guess it does." She fiddled with the napkin roll. "We just happened to run into each other at the hardware store. He helped me pick out the house paint color. I went with one called Sea Glass. It's a pretty light blue-green color. He says he'll pick up the paint for Monday."

"Sounds lovely."

She frowned slightly as she realized Nash

would have to pick up a lot of supplies to do the work on her cottage. "How does Nash get all his supplies here? On the ferry?"

Beverly shook her head. "Sometimes he does take the ferry over. But Nash also has his own boat that he uses to run back and forth when needed. Keeps an old work van parked at the marina to use."

"Makes sense for a contractor doing a lot of work on the island."

"Back to discussing last night." A mischievous smile slipped across Beverly's features. "So after you two picked out the pretty paint color, you two decided to go out on a date to Sharky's?"

Heat flooded her cheeks again. "Oh, no. It wasn't a date." Although... Nash had insisted on paying for their meals. Did that technically qualify their dinner as a date? She quickly pushed that thought aside. "He was just headed to Sharky's and asked me to join him. I think it was just a friendly, neighborly gesture."

Beverly gave her a skeptical smile but didn't argue. "I'm sure. Well, I'll give you a minute to decide on your order."

Jenna blew on the steaming coffee, anxious for her first sip. She glanced up at the board again. So many choices. She finally made a decision and gave Beverly her order. The spinach quiche and a side order of hash browns. Though she was tempted by the peach scone...

She sipped her coffee and looked around the coffee shop. Customers sat chatting and laughing. A woman sat with an infant in her arms, carefully eating her breakfast above the baby's head. Two men had a game of checkers going on between them. One young couple was struggling to keep their toddler in his seat, insisting he sit back down every time he popped up.

Beverly brought her quiche with crisp hash browns on the side, and as she hurried off to wait on another table, Jenna surveyed the bustling coffee shop again. Tables filled with chattering groups and couples, laughter intermingling with the gentle clink of ceramic mugs. For a moment, she felt a pang of loneliness as the sole solitary diner. But it didn't bother her. Mostly.

Back in San Francisco, eating alone had been the norm—hasty bites snatched between assignments or takeout containers consumed at her desk. But here on Magnolia, it appeared that the thing to do was to indulge in companionship over a leisurely breakfast.

Her thoughts drifted to the previous evening, the easy camaraderie she'd shared with Nash over dinner at Sharky's. A small smile tugged at her lips as she recalled their effortless conversation. That had been nice. Easy dinner conversation. She'd make it a point to try and make friends here. Beverly was friendly—although always busy here at the shop when she saw her.

Beverly stopped back by the table. "Can I bring you anything else?"

"No, I'm good."

"Are you busy tonight? The high school drama club is putting on a play this weekend and I have an extra ticket. I always like to go and show my support. We have a few talented student actors and I always enjoy watching the plays they do." Beverly refilled her coffee mug. "Would you like to join us? I'm going with my friend, Maxine. I'm not sure if you've met her yet. She works here at the shop, but I don't think she's been working when you've been in."

"I haven't met her. And I'd love to join you." She smiled, grateful for the invitation to connect with more locals.

"Great. Meet us in front of the theater about six-forty-five. The show starts at seven."

"Thank you. I'll be there. That's nice of you to ask me."

"Got to introduce you to more people here in town if you're going to be a regular." Beverly smiled and headed off to wait on another table.

Jenna sat finishing her coffee, savoring the last few sips as the pleasant hum of conversation surrounded her. It would be nice to get to know other locals and start feeling more at home here.

Jenna arrived at the theater that evening with a few minutes to spare. She certainly didn't want to keep anyone waiting, especially after they had extended such a thoughtful invitation. She stood near the bottom of the steps, taking in the scene as the crowd mingled around her. Groups of friends gathered together, their animated chatter filling the warm evening air. Parents with younger children in tow headed inside, their excitement evident as they anticipated seeing their older sons and daughters perform on stage.

At precisely six-forty-five, Beverly came walking up the sidewalk with another woman at her side. "Jenna, great, you made it." Beverly sent her a warm, welcoming smile. "Maxine, this is Jenna."

Maxine held out her hand. "Great to meet you. I hear you've moved to the island and you're fixing up the old Weston place. Good for you. It certainly needed some love and attention."

Jenna took Maxine's hand, returning the friendly handshake. "I did buy the Weston place, and it needs quite a bit of work. But I absolutely love it. I think it will be wonderful when we're finished with it."

"We?" Maxine raised an eyebrow, a curious expression on her face.

"Oh, I meant Nash and I. Well, not we, as in us. Just I'm doing some work and Nash is doing some work." Jenna felt her cheeks flush slightly as she tried to correct her remarks. She hoped she didn't sound too silly or flustered.

"Yep, we get it." Beverly laughed, her eyes crinkling at the corners with amusement. She gave Jenna a reassuring pat on the shoulder.

The three women stood together for a moment, the easy companionship between them making her feel welcome. All around them, the theatergoers continued to arrive, their anticipation for the evening's performance building. The soft glow of the theater lights spilled out onto the steps, beckoning them inside.

"Oh look. There's Tori." Maxine waved another woman over. "Tori, this is Jenna. New to the island."

Tori gave her a friendly smile. "I'm fairly new myself. You couldn't have picked a better place to settle down. I love it here. Welcome." Her voice was sincere, and Jenna could sense the genuine affection Tori felt for the island.

"Thank you." She wondered how long it took Tori to feel like she fit in.

"Tori restored the theater and got it back up and running," Beverly explained.

"I can't wait to see the kids' production live tonight. They've been rehearsing endlessly. I think you'll really enjoy it," Tori said enthusiastically. Her eyes lit up as she spoke about the upcoming performance, and Jenna could tell that the theater was a true passion for her.

"I'm sure it will be wonderful. I'm just glad you're back open so they can have their productions here again. We should probably go in and grab our seats," Beverly suggested as she started to climb the stairs.

Jenna trailed behind Maxine and Beverly as they entered the theater. The theater was filled with the sound of people talking and laughing. She glanced around, taking in the cozy ambiance as they found their seats. A fleeting glimpse of movement caught her eye—someone quickly peeked out from behind the heavy velvet curtain before vanishing backstage.

An undeniable sense of community ran through the crowd, with familiar faces greeting one another like old friends reuniting. Jenna felt a pang of loneliness wash over her. She suddenly felt lost, adrift in a sea of camaraderie that she wasn't yet a part of.

As Maxine and Beverly delved into an animated discussion about a recent Heritage Festival, their words a whirlwind of unfamiliar traditions and shared memories, Jenna gently shook herself out of her pity party and away from the melancholic thoughts. She'd made this choice to come here to Magnolia and start over. She just needed to give herself time to make friends, that was all.

The lights dimmed, and a quiet anticipation

settled over the theater. With a graceful swish, the velvet curtains parted, revealing the two lead characters poised on stage. As the play unfolded, Jenna found herself immersed in the story, the fact that it was a high school production fading from her mind. The young actors displayed a level of talent that impressed her, proving Beverly's words about the island's artistic community to be true.

When the show ended, she rose to her feet, joining rest of the audience in enthusiastic applause. She and Maxine and Beverly made their way outside and stood in front of the theater. Families lingered, engaging in lively chatter with friends and neighbors.

A man approached the female lead, presenting her with a beautiful bouquet of flowers. The young actress embraced him warmly, exclaiming, "Thank you, Daddy!" Her joy and gratitude were evident in her beaming smile.

Jenna's attention was drawn to a woman approaching them. The woman from the coffee shop—Miss Eleanor—came up to them with a man at her side. Beverly stiffened beside her.

"Evening, Miss Eleanor," Maxine said as she draped her arm protectively around Beverly's waist. Then, turning her gaze to the man,

Maxine addressed him with a chilling intensity. "Cliff…" Her voice carried a hint of warning, and the look she fixed upon him could have frozen the very ocean itself.

The man arched one eyebrow but seemed unaffected by the icy greeting.

"Miss Eleanor, have you met Jenna?" Maxine turned from throwing dagger looks at Cliff.

"Not yet. Welcome to town, Jenna." Miss Eleanor reached out her hand.

Jenna took it, and her hand was enveloped by a surprisingly strong grip. "Thank you."

"This is my son, Cliff. He never did like coming to the shows much. Had to drag him with me tonight. Not much changes."

"No kidding," Beverly said, almost under her breath.

Jenna wasn't sure what was with the undercurrent between everyone, but she didn't miss the glare Beverly sent in Cliff's direction. Cliff promptly returned the glare with a grin.

"We should go. It's getting late," Maxine insisted.

"We should." Beverly nodded and turned to Jenna. "Thank you for joining us tonight. Hope you had a good time."

"I did. It was wonderful. And nice to meet new people."

The crowd began to disperse, and Jenna headed back to her cottage. Walking alone. Not that she was frightened of walking alone at night in Magnolia, and her cottage was just a short distance away. But it would have been nice to have a friendly conversation on her journey home. At least she'd taken the first small step toward making more friends. She'd met Maxine, Tori, Miss Eleanor, and Cliff. Though it was obvious that Maxine and Beverly were not fans of Cliff. Maybe someday she'd hear that story, but for now, it just made her feel more like an outsider.

CHAPTER 6

Jenna spent the next day pulling the faded, peeling wallpaper from the back bedroom walls. She thought a nice pale-yellow shade of paint would brighten up the room. That was something she could do. Her arms ached from the work, and she finally stopped to take a break.

She sat outside sipping on sweet tea and enjoying the gentle breeze coming in off the water. A short distance away, a family had staked their claim on the sandy expanse, a colorful blanket serving as their base camp. Two little girls, all giggles and boundless energy, darted along the water's edge under the watchful eye of their father, never more than a step away.

A jogger went past at a slow, even pace on the hard-packed sand. Two women leisurely strolled down the beach, plucking shells from the sand and dropping into a shared pail. All around her, people savored the unhurried pace of island living.

Jenna exhaled slowly, allowing the tranquil scene to wash over her. She could easily grow accustomed to this pace of life, where moments were meant to be cherished rather than rushed through. Sitting here and just enjoying the moment, her darkest memories seemed to recede, if only temporarily. A joyful peal of laughter from one of the young girls yanked her attention back to the present. The girl's father playfully tossed her into the air, her delighted squeals aloft on the breeze.

Her gaze drifted over to the deck, where a loose railing caught her eye. She mentally made a note to add that to the list of repairs. She couldn't wait to have the repairs all finished and settle in. Making the cottage her own, her home.

After finishing her tea, she pushed off the chair and headed back inside, ready to tackle the project again. Her phone rang with a familiar ringtone as she placed the empty glass in the sink. "Hey, Marly."

"Hey, yourself, sis. How are things going in your new home?" Concerned edged Marly's words.

"They are going fine. I'm in the middle of peeling off worn wallpaper. And I found a contractor to help with some of the repairs."

"You did? Great."

"Beverly recommended him. She's the owner of Coastal Coffee. I've gone there a few times for breakfast and she invited me to go with her and her friend, Maxine, to a show at the theater last night."

"Look at you. Making friends already. That makes me feel better. I hate to think of you all alone on the island." The concern was still clear in her tone.

"You don't have to worry about me, Marly. I like it here. It's just what I need. A change. And I am meeting people. And of course, I have the house to keep me busy."

"How's your freelance work coming along?"

"I've done a few articles here and there. And I'm in contact with a Florida travel website. Hoping to do some work for them. I'll figure it out."

"I know you will, but I still worry about you. It's my job." Marly laughed.

"Well, don't. I'm fine."

Marly's deep sigh came through the cell phone speaker. "I'll try not to. But I do miss you. It's not the same without you here." Her sister's voice took on a wistful tone. "I can't just pop over for a chat or suggest we grab a drink after work like we used to."

"After I get the cottage whipped into shape, you can come visit. Boss me around. Critique my decorating choices. You know, the usual stuff."

Marly laughed. "And you know I will."

"Listen, I have to get back to work. I'd like to have all the wallpaper down before Nash gets here." She headed into the back bedroom.

"Nash. Who is Nash?" Her sister's voice filled with undisguised interest.

"The contractor I told you about." She kept her voice nonchalant, knowing any hint of evasiveness would just prompt more questions.

"Oh, I thought maybe you'd already snagged a date with some handsome local."

"No... I..." No way she was telling her sister she'd gone to eat with Nash. There would be endless questions. "Nope, just the contractor

I mentioned coming to start working on the house tomorrow."

"Okay, I'll let you get back to work. But check in soon. Or, you know, I'll badger you mercilessly," her sister teased.

"Bye, Marly." She clicked off the phone. Her sister meant well. And she had to admit she missed her sister too. Not that they really spent a lot of time together in recent years. She'd always been so busy with her job and her investigations.

She pivoted, staring at the one long wall where the dated wallpaper remained untouched. An unbidden sigh escaped her lips. The wallpaper wasn't going to peel itself free, that much was certain.

She wanted Nash to see how hard she was working on getting projects done on the cottage. That she intended to work just as hard as he did. With renewed vigor, she clasped the scraper in her hand. She resolved to not quit until the last strip of wallpaper surrendered its grasp on the wall.

~

Jenna awoke Monday morning, her body still feeling the effects of the grueling work she'd put in the day before. Despite the soreness in her arms, a sense of satisfaction washed over her as she recalled the completed room. She couldn't help but wonder if Nash would take notice of her efforts.

She quickly got dressed and grabbed a cup of coffee. She stood at the sink while eating a piece of toast with strawberry preserves on it. A woman at the market said that a local woman made the preserves and that they were tasty. The woman did not exaggerate. The preserves were awesome. She debated a second piece of toast, but instead poured yet another cup of coffee, glanced around the kitchen to make sure everything was picked up, and walked out into the living room.

A knock sounded, and she hurried over to open the door. Nash stood there with a toolbox in hand and a friendly smile. "Morning."

"Morning." She glanced behind him to see his truck and another one in the driveway.

"I've got painters that are going to start on the outside. I'll start inside if that's okay with you."

"Yes, come in." She stepped aside to let him pass.

He glanced over at the bookcase. "You working on refinishing those?"

"I am."

He nodded. "They'll look nice. You know how to refinish them?"

"I do." She was determined to show him that she did know how to do a lot of repairs and fixing things up.

"I'll head back to the hall bathroom and work on that plumbing, then." He headed down the hallway, but she saw him pause at the doorway of the back bedroom and look inside. Surely he remembered it had been covered in that horrible, fading wallpaper when he'd been here last week…

Hours later, Nash came into the living room as she stood on a ladder putting a finish on an upper shelf. "You've got quite a lot done in here today."

She paused, holding the rag with the finish on it. "It is starting to look nice, isn't it?"

"And you got all that wallpaper down in the back bedroom. Not sure how you finished all that since I was just here a few days ago. That's quite a project."

Pleasure seeped through her that he'd acknowledged her hard work. "I'm going to paint the room a pale yellow. Just need to get some color cards and bring them back here to see what I might like."

"I've got a set in the truck. Want me to go get them?"

"That would be nice." She carefully climbed down the ladder.

Nash headed outside, and she heard him talking to the men working outside. He soon returned with a deck of color cards. "Want some help choosing the shade?"

"Sure, never hurts to have another set of eyes on the choices." She followed him down the hall to the bedroom.

"Let's open these blinds to let in some natural light." Nash headed over to a window.

"I'm getting rid of those blinds, anyway. They're faded and in pretty terrible shape. I want some nice wooden ones." If she could figure that into her budget. But she didn't tell Nash that.

The light streamed into the room, and she held up the colors on the wall. First in the sunlight, and then in the corners. "I kind of like this one called Butter Cream. But this morning sunshine is nice too." She laughed. "I swear the paint companies must do market research into finding the most compelling names for their paints."

"I bet they do." He nodded. "I don't think you could go wrong with either of them. Nice, neutral pale yellows. It will brighten up the room."

"That's what I'm hoping." She stared at the two colors. "I can't decide."

"I'll tell you what. I'll pick up two sample sizes of the colors. You can paint some on the wall and decide."

"That sounds like a good idea." She handed the cards back to him. "Would you like to take a break and have some sweet tea?"

He glanced out the doorway toward the hall bathroom, then turned back to her and smiled. "Sure, can't see why not."

They headed to the kitchen, and she poured them large glasses of tea. They sat at the table and he stretched his long legs out. "Good tea. Looks like you know how to make it properly."

"I had a good friend from Georgia and I served her iced tea once. She practically spat it out. She insisted on teaching me how to make it properly. I admit, her way beats mine. Made it her way ever since."

"Almost as good as my momma's." He winked. "But don't tell her I said so. She thinks no one makes tea anywhere near as good as hers."

Jenna smiled, enjoying the easy conversation. "Your secret is safe with me. I wouldn't dare challenge your momma's sweet tea supremacy."

He chuckled. "Wise decision. She's fiercely protective of her culinary reputation."

"I can only imagine." Jenna took another sip, savoring the perfect balance of sweetness and tea, just like her friend had taught her. "So, how long have you been in the construction business?"

"Officially, about ten to fifteen years now. But I grew up around it, helping my dad out on jobs since I was old enough to hold a hammer." His eyes crinkled at the corners as he reminisced. "I guess you could say it's in my blood."

"That must be nice. Having a family trade to carry on."

"It is, but it's not without its challenges. Trying to live up to my old man's reputation can be tough sometimes. But I do enjoy my job. Love working with my hands. Meeting people. I enjoy seeing a house come alive as I work on it." He leaned back in his chair. "How about you? What do you do when you're not busy fixing up cottages? You said you used to be an investigative reporter. Why'd you give it up?"

His question caught her off guard. "I… Uh… It was a grueling pace. And stressful. And I just… grew tired of it." She looked at him, not ready to share the whole story. "But this life here on the island agrees with me. I haven't felt this capable and content in a long time."

He nodded. "Sometimes we just need a fresh start."

Luckily, he didn't ask any more questions because she wasn't ready to give answers. She just knew she wanted to get as far away from investigative reporting as possible. And it seemed like she had. This life in Magnolia was a welcome change.

"Anyway, you picked a good spot for it." A pensive look crossed his features. "There's something about this place that just feels… healing."

"I'm starting to see that." Jenna glanced around the kitchen, taking in the progress she'd made. "It's a lot of work, but it already feels more like home."

"You've done an impressive job so far." Nash raised his glass in a mock toast. "To new beginnings and sweet tea."

She laughed, clinking her glass against his. "I'll drink to that."

As they sipped their tea, the conversation flowed easily, ranging from local gossip to their favorite spots on the island. Jenna found herself drawn to Nash's warmth and humor, the way he seemed genuinely interested in her thoughts and opinions.

"You know, I never pegged you for a bookworm," he teased, gesturing to the stack of novels on the counter.

Jenna feigned offense. "Hey, don't let the power tools fool you. I've got layers."

"Clearly." Nash grinned. "So, what's your favorite genre?"

"Mystery, hands down. There's something satisfying about piecing together the clues and solving the puzzle."

"Ah, so you're a regular Nancy Drew." His eyes sparkled with mirth.

"More like a Jessica Fletcher, but I'll take the compliment." She smirked.

They continued to chat, the minutes slipping by unnoticed. It wasn't until Nash glanced at his watch that the spell was broken.

"I should probably get back to work." He stood, stretching his arms above his head. "Those pipes won't fix themselves."

Jenna felt a twinge of disappointment, but nodded in understanding. "Of course. Thanks for taking a break with me."

"Anytime." Nash's smile was warm and genuine.

He headed out of the kitchen and she picked up the glasses, rinsed them, and set them in the dishwasher. A wave of contentment washed over her. For the first time in a long time, she felt like she was just where she was supposed to be.

CHAPTER 7

Jenna hummed softly to herself as she bustled around the kitchen, tidying up the few dishes from her breakfast. The rhythmic sound of hammers and saws drifted in through the open window. She loved opening the windows in the morning to let in the fresh air. Once the day warmed up, it was back to air conditioning.

It had been over a week since Nash and his crew began the renovations on her cottage, and Jenna was surprised by how quickly she'd grown accustomed to their presence. The once-quiet house now had a comforting hum of activity, a far cry from the stillness she'd first encountered when she moved in.

As if summoned by her thoughts, Nash appeared in the doorway, stepping forward as he saw her wrestle to open the cabinet with the broken door. He walked over and examined the cabinet door hinges. "Mind if I take a look at this?"

"Not at all. Go right ahead." Jenna stepped aside, watching as Nash methodically worked to adjust the misaligned door. Replacing the screws in the hinge. Opening and closing the door. Adjusting things again.

She watched him work, his skilled hands moving with confidence and precision. There was an effortless grace to his movements that captivated her.

"A-ha, got it!" Nash declared triumphantly, stepping back to survey his work. "That should do the trick. No more sticking doors."

Jenna smiled. "You're a lifesaver. I dreaded having to wrestle with that every time I needed to get into the cabinet. I tried to fix it on my own, but I'm afraid I just made it worse."

"Happy to help." He offered her a friendly grin, his blue eyes sparkling with satisfaction. "If you're done in the kitchen for a while, I'd really like to replace the pipe that goes to the dishwasher. I noticed there was a bit of moisture at one of the connections. Better to fix it now than wait for a full-out leak. Thought I might work on that next."

"That would be wonderful, thank you. I sure don't want to deal with a leak along with all the other repairs. Just let me fill the coffeepot. Going to make us a fresh pot." And it wasn't the worst thing having him hanging around here.

As Nash disappeared beneath the sink, Jenna busied herself making a fresh pot of coffee, glancing over at him occasionally. The easy camaraderie they'd developed over the past week was a welcome change from the isolation she'd felt when she first arrived.

"There we go." Nash emerged, wiping his hands on a rag. "Should be good as new. Let me know if you have any more issues."

"I will, thanks." Jenna poured him a cup of coffee, black, just the way he liked it. He'd gotten in the habit of taking a coffee break with her mid-morning most days.

"Thanks," he said, taking a sip. "Couldn't do this job without my mid-morning caffeine fix."

Jenna laughed. "I'm happy to keep you fueled up. Wouldn't want you to run out of steam."

Their eyes met, and Jenna felt a spark of something pass between them. She quickly looked away, busying herself by wiping down the countertops. A chore that she'd already done, but he didn't know that.

"So, what's on the agenda for today?" Nash leaned one hip against the kitchen counter.

"Well, I was hoping to tackle painting the back bedroom. I'd love to get that room all painted and set up. My sister wants to come visit, and I'm going to make that the guest room."

"Sounds like a plan." His gaze lingered on her, and Jenna felt her cheeks grow warm under his scrutiny.

"I, uh, I should probably get started then." She hurried down the hallway to the bedroom.

She carefully covered the wooden floorboards with a drop cloth and set out her paint supplies. As she began rolling the paint onto the walls, she glanced out the window and saw Nash, who had joined his crew outside. She allowed herself a moment of watching him work, his muscles flexing beneath his t-shirt. Not that she really noticed, of course.

She sighed, acknowledging she was treading on dangerous ground, allowing herself to be drawn to this charming contractor. But there was something about Nash that made her want to take a chance, to open herself up to the possibility of…

Of what? That was the question, wasn't it?

She turned back to the task at hand, rolling the pale-yellow paint on the wall. When she'd gotten the first coat on the long wall, she moved over to the wall with the closet on it. She'd have to concentrate while she cut in around the closet, then she could go back to rolling.

She dipped her paintbrush in the paint and carefully drew it along the trim of the closet. She stepped back to survey her work, and her foot caught on a loose floorboard.

Jenna gasped as she lost her balance and went crashing to the floor, taking the ladder down with her. Pain shot through her ankle as it twisted beneath her.

"Jenna!" Moments later, Nash came rushing into the room, dropping to his knees beside her. "I heard a crash. Are you alright?"

"I… I think I twisted my ankle," she said, wincing as she tried to move it.

Nash gently examined her ankle. His brow creased in concern. "It's probably just a sprain. Let me help you up." He slid one arm around her waist, supporting her as he guided her to a sitting position.

Jenna leaned into him, grateful for his steady presence. "I'm so embarrassed. I should have been more careful."

"Don't be." Nash's voice was gentle. "I saw that floorboard was loose. I should have fixed it already. You shouldn't have to worry about tripping hazards in your own home. "

"You can't do everything all at once."

"It obviously was a safety hazard. Should have been on the top of my list." The look on his face showed he was clearly annoyed with himself. His arm tightened around her waist. "Can you stand? Let me help you over to the bed."

Jenna nodded, and with Nash's support, she gingerly got to her feet, wincing as she put weight on her injured ankle. He guided her to the bed, helping her sit down carefully.

"There, that's better." He knelt down and gently probed her ankle. "It's starting to swell a bit. Let me get some ice for that."

As he hurried out of the room, Jenna let out a shaky breath. She couldn't believe she'd been so clumsy. And in front of Nash, no less. She'd been trying so hard to prove herself capable of handling this part of the renovation on her own.

Nash returned with a bag of ice wrapped in a towel. "Here, put this on your ankle. It should help with the swelling."

Jenna gratefully accepted the ice pack. "Thank you. I'm sorry for the trouble."

"Don't apologize." He sat down next to her on the bed. "I'm just glad you're not seriously hurt." He reached out and gently squeezed her hand. "Can't have you falling and getting hurt on my watch."

Her heart fluttered in her chest. But it was probably just because of the fall—not because of his touch.

"I'm going to fix that board right now. Let me grab my toolbox." Nash stood and left the room. The room that suddenly felt so very empty.

Come on, Jenna. Get a grip.

He came back with his toolbox and moved over to the loose floorboard, carefully starting to pry it up.

Jenna watched him work, admiring the way his muscles moved beneath his shirt yet again. She blushed when he looked up and caught her staring at him. He just gave her a little smile and continued working on prying the board.

With a final tug, he pulled the board loose. "Well…" He looked up at her, his eyes full of surprise. "That's unexpected."

"What?" She struggled to get on her feet.

"No, don't get up. I'll bring it to you." He reached into the opening and pulled something out. He held up a wooden box tied closed with a now faded ribbon. "Looks like that was someone's secret hiding place."

He carried the box over to her and sat on the bed again with the mysterious wooden container between them.

"I wonder who left it there," Nash mused thoughtfully.

"I don't know." Jenna traced a finger over a carving of a magnolia on the top of the box.

"Go ahead, open it," he urged her.

With a gentle tug, the ribbon fell apart in her hands. She gently opened the box, peering inside. "Oh, look. Letters. And an old photograph." Carefully, she lifted the photo, her eyes drinking in the details. It was a black-and-white image of a couple standing close together, their hands intertwined. Judging by their attire, it was likely from the 1920s. The man gazed down at the woman with a wide, affectionate smile, while she returned his adoring gaze.

"Anything on the back?" Nash peered over to see the photo.

She flipped it over. "No, unfortunately, not." She picked up the stack of letters.

"You going to open them?"

"I don't know... Someone went to great lengths to hide them." And besides, hadn't she sworn off investigating anything ever again? She didn't need to be looking into who hid these items. She needed to be working on the house.

"Well, they're yours to do with what you want." Nash stood. "But I'm going to get that floorboard back in place and make sure it's all even so we don't have any more falling incidents. You stay put until I'm finished and I'll help you out to the living room. I'll clean up the paintbrush and put the top back on the paint can. I think your painting time is over, at least for today."

She sighed. "You're probably right. I should elevate my ankle and stay off of it for a bit."

Nash worked on the board until it was back in place to his satisfaction, then he cleaned up her paint mess. He came over to the bed and held out a hand. She stood up carefully and started to take a step. A wobbly step.

He wrapped his arm around her waist. "Here, lean on me."

She leaned on him, feeling safe and protected as he led her into the living room and settled her on the couch. She stretched out on the couch and put her leg up, adjusting the ice bag back on her ankle. "Thanks. For helping me. For cleaning up after me. And for fixing that board."

"It was nothing." He sent her an easy smile. "I'm just sorry I didn't fix the board before you took your tumble."

"It's fixed now. I'll try not to be so clumsy in the future. I'm... I'm glad you were here."

Nash's blue eyes held hers for a moment. "I'm glad I was here too."

A connection tugged between them. Something more than just a contractor and his client. She didn't know exactly what it was. But there was something there.

"I've got to get back outside and replace some trim. You going to be okay?"

"I'll be fine."

He nodded and walked out the door. She adjusted her seating position to try to see him out the window, but there was no sign of him from where she was sitting. Probably for the best. She couldn't just sit here and stare at him all day. Though she had to admit it sounded like a lovely way to spend the afternoon...

Yes, she knew she was treading on dangerous ground, but in that moment, she couldn't bring herself to care.

CHAPTER 8

Nash checked on Jenna at least every hour throughout the rest of the day, his concern for her outweighing her insistence she was fine. Despite her protests that she could take care of herself, he brought her a sandwich to eat and some tea, making sure she was comfortable and had everything she needed.

As the afternoon wore on, Nash decided to check on Jenna once more. When he entered the living room, he found the couch empty, and a twinge of worry settled in his chest. "Jenna?" he called out, his voice echoing through the quiet house.

"Back here," came her reply, guiding him down the hallway.

He followed the sound of her voice and

found her in the guest bedroom, standing with a paintbrush in hand. Relief washed over him, seeing that she had at least wrapped an ace bandage around her injured ankle. However, the relief was short-lived as he saw her wince when she took a step.

"What are you doing?" His words came out more accusatory than he'd meant for them to.

She looked up at him in defiance. "I thought I'd at least finish cutting in around the closet, the door, and the windows." She shifted her stance, and he noticed her wince again.

He shook his head, a mixture of admiration for her tenaciousness and exasperation at her stubbornness. "Jenna, you need to rest that ankle. Pushing yourself too hard will only make it worse."

"I can't just sit on the couch and do nothing."

Nash sighed. "Yes, you can. The painting will wait for another day." He reached out, hoping to take the paintbrush from her hand.

She snatched it away from his grasp, her face wrinkling with pain as she stepped away from him. She let out a long breath. "Okay, you're probably right. I should rest my ankle."

He reached for the paintbrush again. "Here, I'll go clean that up."

"No, I've got it. I know you have work to do outside." Her look was more one of dismissal than anything else.

He searched her face, wishing she'd let him help her. "Then you'll rest?"

"Then I'll rest again. I promise." Though she darted a glance over to the uncut-in window.

A slight smile tugged at the corners of his mouth as he shook his head. "I'll be back in to check on you."

"Of course you will. You need to make sure you get your check-ins up to an even dozen." She rolled her eyes.

He grinned at her as he walked out the door, unable to resist one last quip. "Only three more times to make that dozen," he called over his shoulder as he headed back outside, determined to finish replacing the trim on the back window so the painters could paint it.

As he measured and cut the boards, his thoughts kept popping back to Jenna. She was one stubborn—okay, a nicer word might be determined—woman. He admired that about her, even if she exasperated him by not staying off her ankle like he'd suggested. In truth, it was more like he told her what to do. She probably didn't appreciate that. She was clearly an independent woman.

The next time he checked on her, she was sitting on the couch, working on her laptop. He brought her another glass of iced tea.

"That's *one* more time." That was all she said to him as she concentrated on her work.

Later, he went in and she held up a hand. "I'm fine."

He turned and walked back out and started back to work. When he'd finished, he stood back and wiped the sweat from his brow as he surveyed the newly installed trim around the back window. Satisfied with his work, he gathered his tools and headed back inside.

He was pleased to find her reclining on the couch, her injured ankle propped up on a pillow. "Can I get you anything? How about I go out and pick you up something for dinner?" He couldn't shake his protective instinct after her fall.

Jenna shook her head. "I'm going to make something simple, like pasta. I'll be fine."

He wasn't convinced, but it was clear there was no use arguing with her. He frowned. "You have my cell phone if you need anything. Call me."

"I'll be fine," she repeated. Then she looked up at him and grinned. "An even dozen check-ins today. Impressive."

He laughed. "Couldn't help myself. You took quite a tumble, and even though you say you're fine, I know that ankle has to ache."

"A bit. I'll take some aspirin before bed if it's still bothering me."

"If you're sure you don't need anything, I guess I'll go." But he didn't want to go. Didn't want to leave her here all alone.

She gave him a shooing motion. "Go. You've put in a long day."

"You're sure."

She sighed in exasperation. "Don't make me say I'm fine again."

He nodded. "Okay, I'm leaving. But call—"

"If I need anything. I know."

He didn't miss her rolling her eyes at him yet again. He reluctantly walked to the door and took one last glance at her before heading out to his truck. Seemed wrong to leave her alone and injured.

He sighed heavily as he climbed into his truck, still feeling unsettled at leaving Jenna. But then, she was one of the most capable women he'd met. She probably didn't need—or want—him hovering over her. But the protectiveness lingered, and he vowed to pick up breakfast for her at Coastal Coffee on his way back to work tomorrow.

But by tomorrow, she'd probably be insisting she was ready to run a marathon. He scowled, thoroughly vexed by her.

Vexed. One of his grandfather's words. Funny how those words would just pop into his mind sometimes. Do people even use the word vex anymore?

He could almost hear his grandfather lecturing him. "Leave the woman alone. She'll ask for help if she needs it."

But would she? He was fairly certain his phone would never ring with a call from her.

Jenna exhaled slowly and gently set her laptop on the coffee table. Nash's hovering had started to annoy her. And yet, it was kind of charming in a way. But she couldn't have him thinking she was some kind of weak damsel in distress.

Determined to prove her point, she gingerly

eased herself off the couch, grimacing as her injured foot made contact with the floor. She surveyed the expanse between her and the kitchen, steeling herself for the journey. With cautious steps, she hobbled across the room, a dull ache radiating through her ankle.

As she navigated the short distance that now felt like miles, a twinge of regret poked at her, making her wonder if perhaps she should have accepted Nash's offer to bring her dinner. But her stubborn pride propelled her forward, unwilling to concede defeat.

She filled a pot with water, set it on the stove, and then rummaged through the pantry until she found a box of pasta. A simple dish of pasta tossed with olive oil, vinegar, and a sprinkle of seasoning sounded perfect for her current mood and energy level. As an afterthought, she decided to add some parmesan cheese on top for an extra burst of flavor.

While the pasta bubbled away on the stove, she leaned against the counter, favoring her uninjured foot. She absently watched the steam rise from the pot, lost in thought, as she waited for the pasta to cook. The timer's sudden beep jolted her back to the present, and she carefully hobbled over to the sink to drain the al dente noodles.

How come whenever she made pasta, there was always too much? Estimating the right amount of pasta had never been her strong suit, but at least she'd have leftovers to reheat later.

She took her bowl over to the table and sank gratefully onto a chair, glad to be off her feet. She was about to dig in when she realized she had forgotten to pour herself a drink. With a resigned sigh, she pushed herself up from the chair and limped to the cabinet, selecting a wine glass. She then opened the fridge and retrieved a chilled bottle of Pinot Grigio, pouring a generous glass before making her way back to the table.

When she'd finished her meal, she put her bowl in the dishwasher, the extra pasta in the fridge, and took her wine glass out to the living room. She plopped down on the couch and looked around the room, feeling restless, not wanting to just sit there doing nothing. She could read—if she got up and got a book. She could watch TV, but she really wasn't much of a television enthusiast. She frowned as another idea sprang into her mind.

She could get the box Nash found in the

guest bedroom. Just to look at the photo again. Nothing more.

She limped down the hallway, grabbed the box, and made her way back to the couch, her curiosity growing with each wobbling step. After settling onto the welcoming cushions, she slowly opened the lid to the box and took out the vintage photograph with care.

She traced a finger over the faded print, studying the faces of the couple captured in a moment of happiness. Who were these people? What was their story? Her gaze drifted to the bundle of letters tucked beneath the photograph, their presence tantalizing. If she read them, she might be able to uncover the identity of the writer and return these mementos to their rightful heirs. Surely, the family would cherish this glimpse into their ancestors' lives, wouldn't they? The temptation to dig into the mystery was hard to resist.

Jenna's fingers hovered over the box, her conscience warring with her curiosity. *No, just leave it alone,* she chided herself, setting the box down and carefully placing the vintage photograph back inside. She leaned back against the couch cushions, her uninjured foot tapping a gentle rhythm on the floor as her gaze wandered around the cozy living room. Despite her best efforts to distract herself, her attention kept drifting back to the mysterious box and the secrets it might contain.

Her curiosity won, and with a resigned sigh, she reached for it again, her pulse quickening in anticipation.

One letter. She'd read just one letter. That couldn't hurt anything, could it? Gently, she unfolded the first letter, the fragile paper crackling softly beneath her fingertips. As her eyes began to scan the elegant, faded script, she felt herself being drawn into the past.

My Dearest,

I'm so grateful you found a way to safely receive my letters. It seems like an eternity since I've seen you. Held your hand. Listened to your laughter.

It is so hard to be here so far away from you. My heart broke into tiny jagged pieces, as sharp as the point of sea glass we found, as my ship pulled away from the island and you got smaller and smaller until I could no longer see you. I don't know when I'll be able to make it back to the island, but I promise you I will return. But just know that my love for you is real. I'll miss you with every breath I take.

All my love forever

Jenna studied the letter, searching for a signature or any clue to the writer's identity, but found none. Carefully, she examined the envelope, hoping for an address or name that might shed light on the mystery, yet it too offered no answers. So many questions swirled in her mind. How did this letter find its way here, seemingly untouched by the passage of time, without any indication of its intended recipient? And who had written these heartfelt words, their love and longing poured onto the page, yearning for a reunion with the one they loved on this very island? She couldn't even tell if the author was a man or a woman, their true self hidden behind the eloquent script.

A twinge of guilt washed over her as if she had eavesdropped on their private conversation, and she gently returned the letter to the box. She pondered the fate of the mysterious writer and the recipient, wondering if they had ever made their way back into one another's arms.

The answers to her questions might lie within the other letters, each one a piece of the puzzle waiting to be uncovered. The temptation to dig deeper into the unknown love story tugged at her curiosity, the allure of unraveling the secrets held within those pages growing stronger with each passing moment. The familiar tug of needing to know the truth poked at her, just like when she was deep into an investigation.

She'd leave the letters alone. They weren't hers to read.

And hadn't she made a promise to herself? A vow born from the painful lessons of her past, to never again interfere in the lives of others. The last time she'd insisted on uncovering the truth at any cost, it had nearly destroyed someone's life. She'd learned the hard way that sometimes, not everything was as it seemed.

She firmly closed the lid. No more reading letters or trying to figure out who wrote them. They were not her business.

With a sigh, Jenna pushed herself up from the couch, her body suddenly heavy with exhaustion. The day's events had taken their toll, and all she wanted was to retreat to the comfort of her bed and rest her injured ankle.

As she made her way back to her bedroom, she flicked off the lights, casting the cottage into darkness. She paused briefly at the guest room door, peering inside at the splash of moonlight spilling across newly repaired flooring. Thanks to Nash's handiwork, there was no trace of the hidden compartment that had once held the box of letters. It was just an empty guest room.

The silence of the cottage overwhelmed her as she entered her bedroom. She turned on some soft, soothing music on her phone and let the gentle melodies fill the space as she got ready for bed. She crawled beneath the covers, then reached for the book on her nightstand in the hope that it might provide a welcome distraction from the thoughts that plagued her. With any luck, she would get lost in the story.

The book was good, the story compelling, but still thoughts of the mysterious couple danced in the recesses of her mind.

CHAPTER 9

Jenna's ankle throbbed the next morning as she eased herself out of bed, but she refused to let it stop her. Determined to make more progress on the guest room, she wrapped her ankle with the bandage again, securing it tightly. She limped into the kitchen, greeted by the aroma of freshly brewed coffee. Nothing better than an automatic coffee maker that welcomed her every morning with her much-needed coffee.

She grabbed a quick breakfast and then moved to stand by the window, sipping her second cup of coffee. A brisk breeze whipped up the waves, and whitecaps dotted the expanse of water. Waves danced restlessly to shore, curving with frothy curls before crashing onto the beach.

She checked the weather app on her phone and saw that a storm was predicted for later this afternoon.

As she cleared up her breakfast dishes, she heard the voices of the men coming to work on her house. Nash had told her that some of the gutters needed replacing. The list just kept growing longer. But she was still convinced it was going to be a lovely cottage when all the work was finished.

She spotted Nash on the deck, already hard at work on the railing. She opened the door and called out a greeting. "Morning."

He turned around and an immediate smile flashed on his face. "Good morning. Wasn't sure if you'd sleep in this morning. How's the ankle?" He motioned toward her foot.

She dragged her gaze from staring at his eyes and his smile and glanced down at her ankle. "Aches a bit, but it's better. I've wrapped it so I can finish painting the guest room today."

His brow creased with concern. "You sure you should do that? Wouldn't hurt to stay off of it another day or so."

"I'll be fine." Probably. At least she was going to give it a try.

He shot her a skeptical look but didn't try to

convince her to rest. No doubt he'd figured out how stubborn she could be.

"I'll see you for a coffee break mid-morning?" she offered, hoping to appease him somewhat.

He nodded, still frowning.

She turned and headed back toward the bedroom. She got out the brush to finish cutting in around the closet and windows, carefully and precisely starting in on the task. Her ankle started to ache more, but she ignored it, determined to work on the project.

Later, Nash's deep voice startled her from her concentration. "Hey, you about ready to take that break?" His eyes were filled with concern. How long had he been standing there watching her? Had he seen her wincing with each step?

She glanced at her watch, surprised to see how much time had passed. "Sure, that sounds good." She set the roller on the paint tray and covered it with a plastic bag. That would keep it for now.

She followed Nash to the kitchen. "Coffee should still be hot in the insulated pot."

"How about I get it? You go sit on the couch and put that ankle up for a bit."

"Pretty bossy today, aren't you?" She shook her head, but smiled. "I'm fine. But, just to please you, I'll go and sit down."

She limped over to the couch and sat down, propping her foot on a pillow to relieve some of the dull ache. Moments later, Nash entered the living room, carrying two steaming mugs of coffee. He handed one to her, and she accepted it gratefully, savoring the warmth against her hands, tired from gripping the paint roller.

He settled into the chair across from her and motioned toward the wooden box resting on the coffee table. "So, did you decide to look at the letters?"

"I... I did. I read one of them." She frowned, still remembering how she'd wavered back and forth on whether she should look at them. "But then... then I felt like I was peeping into their lives. Invading their privacy. So I put it back."

"What did the letter say?"

"It was kind of a love letter. Whoever wrote it was leaving the island and saying how much they'd miss whoever they wrote to." She paused, tracing the rim of the mug with her finger. "Oh, and something about finding a way to get the letters safely delivered. I'm not sure what that was about."

He raised an eyebrow. "Aren't you curious to find out more?"

She smiled self-consciously, her gaze dropping to the wooden box on the coffee table. "I am a bit. But I still feel like it's not really my right to pry into their private correspondence."

"What if you could find out who wrote them and get them back to their heirs? That would be the right thing to do, wouldn't it?"

She chewed her bottom lip, a flicker of temptation poking her. "But if they went to all these lengths to keep a secret, maybe they wouldn't want their family to know."

"Good point." Nash nodded. "But... maybe it wasn't a secret that needed to be kept forever."

"Maybe." But the nagging voice of her former investigative instincts begged her to leave it alone. And hadn't she promised herself not to go looking into things that didn't concern her? No more investigating.

"I could help you try and figure it all out. Figure out who wrote the letters and who's in the picture," he offered.

It did tempt her to work on it with him, but

she still wasn't sure she should even be reading the letters. She shook her head slowly. "I don't know."

"Well, if you change your mind, let me know."

"I will."

"I saw you got another wall of the guest room painted. Are you pleased with your choice of color?"

"I am. It really makes the room more cheerful. After I get finished, I think I'll order new window treatments and a new bedspread. Spruce the room up a bit. I'd like a dresser for in there too."

"There's a great second-hand shop here in town, Second Finds. It's owned by Dale, a local. He refinishes furniture he finds. He has some nice things in there."

"I'll take a look. Thanks for the recommendation."

Nash stood. "I better get back to work. Want to see how much we can get finished outside before the storms come in."

She glanced out the window at the clouds. "I should get back to my painting while I still have some good natural light in the room."

"Or… you could rest." He eyed her sternly,

but his eyes twinkled, like he knew he'd already lost that battle.

She rolled her eyes at him. "But, I'm not going to."

He chuckled. "Of course you're not." Giving her one more smile, he headed back outside.

She finished her coffee and then got back to work. The room darkened as the storm inched closer. She finally had to turn on the overhead fixture, but the puny light didn't really give her good enough illumination to paint. It was a good time to quit. And besides, her ankle was throbbing steadily now, not that she'd admit it.

Nash glanced up as the thunder crashed in the distance. Lightning flashed over the sea, illuminating the waves crashing to shore. He quickly gathered his tools, glad he'd sent the other workers home earlier. Just then the heavens opened up and poured down the fury of Mother Nature. He was drenched within moments.

The next flash of lightning illuminated Jenna, standing at her door, motioning him to come inside. "Hurry. Come in out of the storm." Her voice was nearly drowned out by the wind and the pounding rain.

He grabbed his toolbox and sprinted for her door, stepping inside out of the downpour. Water puddled around him. "I'm sorry. Afraid I'm making a mess."

"That's no problem. It will clean up. Let me get you a towel." She disappeared and came back with a white, fluffy towel.

He took it and tried to dry himself off as best he could.

"If you give me your shirt, I'll toss it in the dryer."

He shucked off the shirt self-consciously, very aware of Jenna's gaze lingering on his bare chest. When she finally met his eyes again, a faint blush tinted her cheeks before she quickly averted her stare.

She cleared her throat. "I'll get you a shirt to wear."

"I'm pretty sure I'm not your size." A grin tugged at the corner of his mouth.

She paused, as if flustered by his playful quip. "I sleep in large t-shirts. I'll grab you one." With that, she turned and disappeared down the hallway.

He watched her go, imagining her padding around the cottage in an oversized t-shirt. He shook his head at his thoughts. Getting distracted by fantasies about his client was unwise, no matter how enticing the prospect. He needed to rein in his unruly imagination before it led him down a path that might not be such a smart one to take.

She reappeared, clutching an oversized Giants t-shirt in her hands. Nash accepted it with a smile, and his fingers grazed hers as he took the soft, well-worn fabric. "You a baseball fan?" he asked, amused by the logo emblazoned across the front.

"Nope, not at all. My sister is, and she gave me that in hopes I'd become one too. It didn't work, but the shirt is soft and one of my favorites to sleep in." She shrugged.

Slipping the shirt over his head, he caught the delicate scent of fabric softener. He drew in a deep breath as the soft fabric settled against his skin. "Now let me mop up this mess."

"I'll get it," she insisted, already turning toward the kitchen.

He reached out, his hand circling her wrist to stop her. "No, I insist. And you should be off that ankle anyway," he teased. "It's been hours since I've been able to nag you about it."

Rolling her eyes good-naturedly, she pulled away. But not before he'd felt the warmth of her skin beneath his palm. "So glad you came in to boss me around again." Her lips curved into a smile as she walked away and returned with a mop.

Wordlessly, he set to work sopping up the puddles, careful to thoroughly dry each plank of the hardwood floor. When the last drops disappeared, he straightened with a satisfied nod. "I think I got most of it."

"I really need to get some rugs for in front of the doors. Just haven't had time." She took the mop back, her fingers brushing his as she did. A deafening crash of thunder shook the cottage, and she jumped. She sent him a tiny smile when she recovered.

"Looks like we're getting quite the storm." He glanced out the window. Rain pelted the glass, and the wind howled outside.

"It is quite the storm. You should stay until it eases up some."

"Thanks, don't mind if I do." There was no use getting out on the roads with a storm like this. That was the only reason he'd agreed with her. Not because he wanted to spend more time with her. Of course not.

He followed her into the kitchen and she put the mop away.

The lights flickered momentarily, casting the room in fleeting shadows before the warm glow returned. "You got candles?" He glanced around the kitchen.

"I do. I remembered how the electricity would often go out in the storms here on the island, so I picked some up." She opened a drawer, revealing a neat row of thick pillar candles and a box of matches.

"Lanterns, candles, batteries, bottled water. Food to eat that doesn't need to be cooked. Always need a supply of them all. Especially during hurricane season."

She frowned, her eyes clouding with uncertainty. "Never been here during hurricane season. Is it bad?"

Leaning back against the counter, Nash considered how to explain the cold, harsh realities of life on the island during hurricane season without alarming her too much. "Sometimes," he admitted. "Most people leave the island and seek shelter on the mainland if one is headed this way. The ferry shuts down, so you'd be stranded if you stay."

Her frown deepened as she processed his words. "I never even thought of that when I bought this place."

He gave her a reassuring smile and reached out to give her shoulder a comforting squeeze. "It's just part of island life." He realized his hand was still resting on her shoulder and he quickly took it back. "Anyway, we can just enjoy being all snug and inside while this storm blows through."

Just then, the lights flickered, and they were plunged into darkness. Jenna clicked on the flashlight on her phone and pulled out some candle holders from the cabinet. He helped her light the candles and place them in the holders. The candles threw flickering shadows around the kitchen.

"Are you hungry? We could make us a snack." She turned to him.

"That sounds good."

He sliced up the apples she handed him while she put together a plate with cheese and crackers. She poured them each a glass of wine. The domestic atmosphere of the moment wasn't lost on him. It felt natural, comfortable, being here with her like this.

They carried their impromptu picnic into the living room, setting everything on the coffee table. Nash settled onto the couch, acutely aware of Jenna's proximity as she sat down beside him. The candlelight softened her features, highlighting the glow of her skin.

"This is nice," she said, taking a sip of her wine. "Almost makes me glad the power went out."

He chuckled. "There's something to be said for slowing down, taking a break from the constant buzz of electricity and screens."

She nodded, selecting a slice of apple from the plate. "I've been so focused on getting the cottage fixed up, I haven't taken much time to just... be. And I specifically moved here to slow down."

"It's important to do that, to find those moments of peace amid all the chaos of daily life." He reached for a cracker, his fingers brushing hers. A tingle raced up his arm at the contact.

They chatted easily as they nibbled on their snacks, the conversation flowing from their shared love of the island to childhood memories to hopes for the future. The cozy atmosphere felt like they were the only two people in the world.

Nash found himself opening up to her in a way he rarely had with anyone else. There was just something about Jenna that made him feel at ease, made him want to share his thoughts, his dreams.

As the evening wore on, the candles burned lower, casting intimate shadows around the room. He became increasingly aware of the subtle attraction simmering between them. The way Jenna's gaze would linger on his a beat too long, the way his own eyes were drawn to the curve of her lips as she spoke.

He set his wineglass down as he suddenly realized, with crystal clear clarity, that he was beginning to develop feelings for her. Feelings that went beyond the simple desire to help a newcomer settle into life on the island. No, this was something deeper.

How could that happen when he'd only known her for such a short time?

And he hesitated to act on those feelings, unsure if Jenna felt the same way. The last thing he wanted was to make her uncomfortable or jeopardize their budding friendship. So he convinced himself he was content with simply enjoying her company, enjoying their conversation as the storm raged on outside.

Eventually, the wind died down, and the rain tapered off to a gentle patter against the windows. Nash knew he should probably head home, but he was reluctant to leave the cozy bubble they'd created. "I should probably get going," he said grudgingly, setting his empty wineglass on the table. "It's getting late."

Jenna nodded, a flicker of disappointment crossing her face. "I suppose so." She walked him to the door, the candlelight casting a soft glow over her features. "Thanks for staying, Nash. It was really nice having company during the storm."

"Anytime," he said, maybe a bit too enthusiastically. "And, truly, if you ever need anything, just let me know. You know, besides just helping you with your home."

She smiled, and for a moment, he thought he saw a reflection of his own longing in her eyes. But then it was gone, and she was opening the door, the cool night air rushing in to replace the warmth of the cottage.

"If it's raining tomorrow, we won't be here.

Going to work on another project where the work is all indoors."

She nodded—and was there a bit of disappointment in her eyes?

With a final goodbye, he stepped out into the darkness. His heart was full of uncertainty, knowing he would have to tread carefully, to let things develop naturally between them. That is, if she was beginning to feel the same way about him as he felt about her.

He let out a sigh as he climbed into his truck. Relationships were complicated.

CHAPTER 10

Later that evening, Jenna's phone rang, its cheerful tone echoing through the now empty cottage. She smiled when she saw her sister's photo and clicked on the video call. "Hey, Marly."

"Hi, sis. Hope I'm not calling too late. I'm still trying to get used to the time change between us now."

"Yep, three hours difference. But I'm still up. Nash just left." The words just slipped out, and she instantly regretted her remark.

Marly didn't disappoint, her eyes widening with curiosity. "Nash? The contractor guy? What was he doing there so late?"

"We had a big storm come through. He just

waited it out while it passed. It was a big storm. Electricity went out. It just came back on a few minutes ago.

"So you just sat there in the dark? All alone?" Marly prodded.

"No, I made us a snack. And I had candles, of course. Don't you remember how often the electricity would go out when we visited?" Why, oh why, had she mentioned Nash had stayed with her during the storm? Marly was never going to let it go.

"So you had a romantic meal by candlelight." Her sister's eyes sparkled with mischievousness.

"Marly, you're relentless."

"It's part of my charm. You love me for it." Marly grinned and flipped her hair back with a dramatic flick of her hand.

She rolled her eyes, but she couldn't help smiling. "Marly, seriously. Leave it."

"Okay, I will. For now. So how's the cottage coming along? Give me a video tour."

Grateful for the change of subject, she flipped the camera on the phone and started showing off the cottage. "Here are the bookcases. I've been working on refinishing them, but I'm not done. And here's the kitchen. The cabinets and plumbing are all fixed." She walked around the cottage, showing Marly what they'd been working on. "And here's the guest room. Not finished yet, but it will be and waiting for you to visit."

"Looks nice. And I should visit soon so I can meet this Nash guy."

"Marly..." She headed out to the living room and slowly panned the room for her sister to see.

"What's that box on the coffee table?"

"Oh, there was a loose floorboard and when Nash went to fix it, he found a hidden compartment below the floor. This wooden box was in it." She zoomed in on the wooden box.

"Nash, huh?" Marly didn't even try to hide her grin.

She ignored her sister.

"Anyway, that's cool. What's in the box?" Marly asked.

"A photo of a couple—looks like from the 1920s or so—and a stack of letters." She opened the box and showed the contents to her sister.

"What do the letters say?"

"I only read one. It was a love letter. And whoever wrote it was leaving the island but promised to return."

"Why did you stop at just reading one?"

"I… you know. After what happened with that last investigation, I don't think I should poke around in things that aren't my business." She switched the camera back to face her, done with the impromptu tour.

"You do realize you're an investigative reporter and you were only doing your job." Marly shook her head.

"And I did a poor job of it, didn't I?" She could hear the self-reproach and regret in her voice.

"No, you didn't. It's not your fault. You just reported on what you found." Concern flashed in Marly's eyes.

"And look what that did. And I didn't even uncover the truth. I should have kept going."

"Your boss pulled you off the story, right? He told you to move on to the next one," Marly reminded her gently.

"But I should have kept digging. I felt like I didn't have all the pieces."

"You need to forgive yourself, Jenna. You were doing your job, and you did the best you could with what you had." Marly's words were filled with understanding and support.

Jenna hobbled over to the couch, a wave of exhaustion washing over her. The emotional toll of the conversation, combined with the physical strain of her injury, left her feeling drained.

Marly frowned. "Hey, are you limping?"

"A bit. Twisted my ankle."

"Are you okay? You should put your foot up."

Oh, good. When Nash wasn't here nagging her about putting her foot up, her sister could step in and take his place. She sighed as she settled on the couch and propped her throbbing ankle up. "You satisfied?"

"You should be more careful."

"I tripped on that loose board. The one that was covering the hiding space for the box."

"You know, maybe you should read these letters. Maybe you can figure out why they were hidden there. And if you solve the mystery, maybe it will help you heal from what happened before. Because you do need to move on, Jenna. You do."

"I have. I've moved to Magnolia Key."

"No, sis, you ran away to Magnolia Key. That's totally different."

"Can we not go over this again?"

"Okay, but I still think you should read the letters. You're a great investigator. It's a piece of the island's history. Some kind of secret relationship. Hey at the very least, you might dig up some juicy island gossip. Aren't you the least bit curious? "

"I am. But still, they went to great lengths to hide this box."

"Maybe it just got misplaced, or they didn't have time to retrieve it because a hurricane came in and they left. I bet you could come up with lots of theories. You won't know unless you look into it. Maybe their family would love to have this piece of history."

"That's what Nash said." She instantly regretted her remark.

Marly broke into a wide grin. "Oh, he did, did he?"

She let out a long sigh. "He did. And he offered to help me try to figure out who the couple is."

"Now that sounds like a sensible plan. Let Nash help you figure it all out." Marly cocked her head to one side, not bothering to hide her grin. "And that would mean you'd have to spend more time with him."

"Oh, look at the time. It's getting late. I should probably head off to bed."

"Right. You should. But maybe a bit of light reading before bed would be a good idea. Night, sis." And with that, Marly clicked off the call.

She set down her phone and stared at the wooden box, torn with indecision. Maybe... maybe she should read just one more ...

She reached over and opened the box, taking out the stack of letters. She selected one, and the crinkled paper rustled as she unfolded it. The page was worn as if it had been read a hundred times or more.

My Dearest,

Oh, how I miss you and wish I could return. I'm sorry circumstances have prevented us from having the future I wish we could have. My duties keep me here. And I have responsibilities that I can't walk away from, no matter how much I want to.

I know you haven't received a letter from me for a long time. I'm sorry. I was trying to forget about us. And the noble thing would be to just walk away. But I can't bear to have no contact with you.

I just got a packet of your letters and it was so good to hear about your days and what you've been doing. I wish I'd been there to go to the festival with you, just like a normal couple.

But the fates have declared that will never happen for us. I'm not sure why they decided to have us meet, and then so cruelly establish the fact that we, as a couple, are impossible.

I will return though. At least I'll be able to see you again, even if that is all we'll ever get.

All my love forever

This letter was unsigned too. But at least a few more details were revealed. What was keeping the two of them apart? She glanced at the stack of letters and took out the next one. She read a half dozen more, but they didn't reveal much. How was she going to figure out who wrote these? Who was the couple in the photograph?

She looked at the letters spread out before her on the table and checked the time. She should really call it a night. Carefully slipping the letters back into their original envelopes, she placed the letters she'd read on the bottom of the box and the unread ones on top. She'd tackle more of them when she had time.

She headed back to her bedroom, still a bit uncertain if she'd made the right decision to read the letters. She climbed into bed and turned off the lights but could only lie there staring into the darkness, her mind racing with thoughts of Nash intertwined with questions about the couple in the photograph.

CHAPTER 11

Jenna awakened the next morning to a steady, soothing patter of raindrops against her bedroom window. Disappointment tugged at her when she realized the steady drizzle meant Nash likely wouldn't be coming by to work on the cottage today. But he did have other projects that needed to be done. And he'd devoted a lot of his time working on her house. He had other crews at other projects that he surely needed to check on.

She slipped out of bed and padded into the kitchen, the hardwood floors warm beneath her feet. Once she had a steaming mug of coffee cradled in her hands, she wandered over to the window and gazed out at the water. The waves rolled steadily to shore as a group of sandpipers scurried along at the shoreline.

Suddenly, the idea of spending the day all alone at the cottage held absolutely no appeal. Breakfast at Coastal Coffee sounded like a much better idea. Besides, if she hurried, she might get to see Nash there having his breakfast. A tiny flicker of excitement skittered through her at the chance to see him.

With that decided, she got dressed and at the last minute decided to tuck the photograph from the wooden box into her purse. She drove to Coastal Coffee—no way her ankle was up for the walk, even though it was feeling a bit better this morning. Beverly greeted her with a hug. "Not a lot of customers coming out in the rain. Glad you came by though."

Jenna swept her gaze over the room, disappointment sweeping through her when she saw no sign of Nash.

"He just left a few minutes ago." Beverly led her to a table.

"Who?" she asked innocently.

Beverly laughed. "Nash, of course. You were looking for him, weren't you?"

The heat of a blush crept over her cheeks, betraying her flustered state. "I was," she admitted with a sheepish grin. "He's not coming to my cottage today. I thought I might catch him here this morning."

"Let me grab you some coffee and get your order put in. We're slow today. I've got time to sit and chat a bit if you'd like."

"I'd love that."

Soon she was nibbling on thick slices of French toast, the bread soaked in a vanilla-scented batter and griddled to golden perfection. Crispy strips of bacon accompanied the decadent breakfast, their salty crunch providing the perfect complement. Not the healthiest meal, but deliciously indulgent.

Beverly came over and sat across from her, a mug of steaming coffee in her hand. "So, what's new with the fixing up of your cottage?"

"It's coming along great." She set down her fork. "And the strangest thing. I tripped on a loose board in the guest bedroom and when Nash was fixing it, he found a secret compartment below the floorboards. There was a wooden box in it with a black-and-white photo of a couple. And a stack of letters. Lots of letters." She dug in her purse and slid the photo across the table to Beverly. "Do you know who they could be?"

Beverly picked it up and looked at it carefully. "No clue. But it looks like it was from before my time." She looked up. "Do the letters give you any clue? Do you know who wrote them?"

"I have no idea. They aren't signed with any names. I read a few of them, but they didn't give me any clues. And... I felt a bit guilty about reading their correspondence. But then I thought maybe I could figure out who wrote them and return the letters and photo to their family."

"We sure are having a lot of mysteries turn up in this town." Beverly's brow creased. "Not long ago, I found a hidden painting in my office. It's a canvas depicting a building strikingly similar to the one that used to stand by the ferry landing years back. And Maxine found an old letter hidden in a purse."

"Really? I wonder why all these things are turning up now?" She frowned.

"And you'll never believe this—the letter was written in code. And it turns out that Cliff—that's Miss Eleanor's son—knew about the code. It was one his family had used." Beverly paused to take a sip of her coffee. "But that's not all. Tori found an antique locket hidden in a desk at the theater. Found out it was Vera Whitmore's. From back in the 1920s. No one knows why she left it there."

Jenna's mind kicked into overdrive. Were some of these mysteries connected with the wooden box she'd found? The photograph she'd found looked like it was from that era. "That is a lot of unanswered questions."

"Maybe if you read more of the letters, it will give you some more clues. See if any of this ties together."

She nodded thoughtfully. "I wonder if it does tie together in some way." She frowned. But hadn't she sworn off investigating things after the ordeal that had led her to move to Magnolia Key?

"You know what? You should go talk to Dale at Second Finds. He's Maxine's boyfriend. I guess you still call it boyfriend at our age?" Beverly laughed. "Anyway, he's kind of our local historian. He might know something that will help you. Tell him what you found out. He might have ideas on where else to look to figure out who wrote the letters."

"Oh, Nash suggested I go there to look for a dresser for my guest room. Maybe I'll drop by to do that and show Dale the photo while I'm there."

"That's a good idea. If anyone can help you out, Dale can."

She finished her delicious breakfast and headed to the door, the scent of the sea air mixing the with aroma of the fresh brewed coffee as she stepped outside. Though it wasn't far, she got in her car and drove to Second Finds. No use tempting fate with her ankle.

She opened the door to the shop, and the bell jangled as she stepped inside. "Be with you in a minute," a voice called out from the back of the store.

She wandered around the shop, her fingers lightly tracing the smooth surfaces of the refinished furniture. Whoever had restored these pieces clearly possessed talent and an eye for detail.

A man came walking up to her. "Hi, I'm Dale. What can I help you with?"

"Hi, Dale. I'm Jenna."

Recognition dawned in his eyes. "Oh, Jenna. Maxine said you went to the theater with Beverly and her. You're new in town. You bought the old Weston place. Nice to meet you."

"I guess the cottage will forever be known as

the old Weston place." She grinned, already feeling at ease with his warm welcome.

"Probably." He returned her smile. "Old habits die hard here in our small town. Anyway, what brings you in?"

"I'm looking for a dresser for the guest room. Nothing too large. The room isn't that big. And Beverly suggested I show you this photograph I found hidden in the cottage. Ask if you might know who it is." She took out the photo and handed it to him.

Dale took the photograph, studying it intently. The crease between his brows deepened as he scrutinized the faded image. "I can't put a name to the faces off the top of my head, but if you don't mind, I can take a photo of it with my phone. That'll allow me to cross-reference it against some of the old records and photo albums I have tucked away."

"That would be great. I also found a stack of letters, but they haven't given me a clue and they aren't signed. I'm going to go through the rest of them, though, and see if they give me any hints."

"I'll research what I can while you do that. Maybe we can figure something out." He took a quick picture of the photograph with his phone and handed the photo back to her. "Now, you said you were looking for a dresser? I just refinished one, and it's back here. Let me show it to you."

She followed him toward the back of the shop, her eyes widening in delight when she saw the dresser. The rich, cherry wood gleamed in the soft light, and it was indeed the perfect size. "This is absolutely lovely. You do great work, Dale."

"Thanks. I love finding old things and fixing them up. It's so rewarding to bring an old, neglected piece of furniture back to life." Dale beamed with pride.

"I completely understand that feeling. That's how I feel about fixing up my cottage." She ran her finger over the smooth top of the dresser. "I'll take this." She frowned slightly, realizing a potential obstacle. "But I don't have a way to get it to my cottage. I didn't think that far ahead."

"No worries. I can deliver it to you," he reassured her.

"Could you give me a few days to finish painting the room? I want everything ready before I move in any more furniture." She could just picture the exact spot for the dresser.

"Sure, I'll deliver the end of the week if that

works. Write your phone number down for me, and we'll connect to set up a time."

"Thanks, Dale."

She headed back to her cottage, anxious to get back to the painting now. She wanted to get it wrapped up and set up the guest room. And maybe even talk her sister into coming for a visit. Though she'd have to put up with Marly nagging her about Nash...

But it would be good to see her. Show her around the island and what had changed since they'd come here as kids. Introduce her to her new friends. Prove to her that she hadn't *run away*... she'd just chosen a new path in life.

CHAPTER 12

Jenna opened her door that evening, surprised to find Nash standing on the doorstep. He gave her a lopsided smile. "I just thought I'd drop by and check on you. Make sure you were doing okay."

She eyed him. "You mean you wondered if I was staying off my ankle?"

"But you notice I didn't ask." He winked.

"I'm doing fine. Sure was quiet around here today without the workers or a certain contractor pestering me." The corners of her mouth lifted as she tried to hide her smile.

"Bet it was. Did you enjoy the quiet?"

She shrugged. "Not so much. I'd gotten used to having people around." Him around. She'd gotten used to having him around. But she didn't say that.

"I know this is last minute, but would you like to go to a concert at the gazebo this evening? Starts in about an hour. Since the rain stopped this afternoon, it's still on."

His offer surprised her. "I... uh..."

"I should have probably called to ask you. Give you some advance notice." His eyes reflected uncertainty.

Recovering from her fluster, she bantered back, "Mr. Carlisle, are you asking me on a date?"

"What if I am?" He raised an eyebrow playfully.

She pretended to consider it. "I guess I could pencil you into my very open evening calendar."

"Great." He broke into a wide smile.

She wasn't one to usually do things spontaneously, but she couldn't resist spending time with Nash. And was this a date? If a spontaneous one?

He led her out to his truck, and they drove to the town park with the gazebo. He came around and opened the door for her and she slid out, bumping into him as she lost her balance when she forgot to favor her bum ankle. "Oh, sorry."

"Not a problem. I've got you." Nash's voice was warm and reassuring as his strong arm steadied her. "I won't let you fall."

She tried to ignore the small flutter in her chest as she stood there in his protective embrace. As she regained her balance, planting her good foot firmly on the paved path, Nash's arm slipped away. A subtle sense of loss bubbled through her. Which was silly. He was still standing just a few feet from her.

"You all good now?" A faint smile played across his lips, and she felt her cheeks flush slightly under his gaze.

"All good."

He reached into the back of the truck and retrieved a pair of well-used lawn chairs, their fabric faded from countless summers under the sun. "This way," he said, nodding toward the gazebo. She followed him as he navigated through the crowd, his steps sure and steady. He glanced back every few moments, ensuring she was right beside him and managing well on her injured ankle. The gesture, small as it was, filled her with a warmth that had nothing to do with the warm evening air.

People greeted Nash and called out to him, looking at her curiously as they made their way through the crowd. He found a spot near the gazebo and set up their chairs with a practiced ease. She settled beside him and took in the lively scene. On the far side of the crowd, she spotted Beverly, Maxine, and Dale, laughing and chatting with friends. A few other faces looked familiar—the cashier from the grocery store, a couple from the diner—but most were still strangers.

"Quite a turnout," she said as she turned to Nash.

"We do like our festivals and concerts. And it's turned into a perfect night for it, now that the storm has passed."

"Seems like everyone we passed knows you."

"Pretty much." He bumped his shoulder playfully against hers. "Don't worry, soon they'll all get to know you too."

Maybe. But she couldn't shake the nagging uncertainty that whispered in the back of her mind. Would she ever truly belong here, or would she forever feel like an outsider in this close-knit community?

A group of people talking behind them caught her attention. "Did you hear about the locket that they found at the theater? Wonder why it was hidden all these years?"

Another chimed in. "And that painting Beverly found. Sure are a lot of mysterious things happening."

Jenna turned to Nash, her curiosity aroused. "I couldn't help but overhear those people behind us talking about mysterious things popping up around town," she whispered discreetly. "I was talking to Beverly, and she told me about the locket and the painting she found. Oh, and a letter Maxine found. That seems like a lot."

"And your wooden box. Did you read any more letters?"

"I did. But I didn't really learn much. Still don't know who wrote them. But I showed the photo to Dale at Beverly's suggestion. He's going to do some digging around and see if he can find anything out by looking through the records and photos he has."

"Dale is kind of our unofficial historical society here on Magnolia Key." Nash laughed. "If anyone can help shed some light on this mystery, it's Dale. The man knows everything about this island's past."

The music started, and the chattering crowd

quieted down. An assortment of local acts took to the stage. A barbershop quartet charmed with their harmonies, their voices blending like the perfect glass of sweet iced tea. A high school boy strummed his guitar, pouring his heart into every note. An older woman stood alone in the spotlight, her rich alto tones washing over the enraptured audience as she sang a haunting ballad of love and loss.

As the final notes of the concert faded into the night, they rose from their seats and gathered their chairs. Nash slung the straps over his broad shoulder and gently took her elbow, his touch warm and reassuring. "It's getting a bit dark out here. Don't want you falling."

Back at his truck, Nash, ever the gentleman, helped her climb into the passenger seat. The ride back to her cottage was filled with comfortable silence and the soft hum of the engine. When they arrived, he swiftly jumped out and hurried around to open the door for her. She slid out, this time managing to maintain her balance and avoid crashing into him. Which was either good… or bad. Wouldn't have hurt anything to feel his arms around her again.

She chased the thought away and cleared

her throat. "Would you like to come in? I had just opened a bottle of red wine when you showed up earlier this evening. Would you like to have a glass with me?"

"Don't mind if I do."

They went inside and he followed her to the kitchen.

She poured two glasses of the dark red wine, the liquid swirling gracefully in the glass as she handed him one. "Want to head out to the deck? It's such a beautiful night."

They walked outside and settled onto the wooden glider. He stretched out his long legs while she propped her bad ankle up on an ottoman. He smiled approvingly.

"Looks like we missed the sunset," she said as she glanced out at the horizon where the last traces of vibrant oranges and pinks were fading into the inky depths of the evening sky.

"We did. But there will be plenty more. Magnolia Key is known for spectacular sunsets." He nodded and took a sip of his wine, visibly relaxing.

She took a sip of her wine and turned to him. "So, how was your work day? Did you get a lot done?"

"We did. Installed some cabinets in a house

where the owners basically gutted the place and they're having us redo it."

"I hope working on my cottage isn't delaying your job for them."

"Naw, we're good. They won't be back to the island for months, so I have time. We should be back here to work first thing in the morning."

That pleased her. One day of quiet had been enough. Though isn't that why she'd moved here to Magnolia? For the slower life and the peace and quiet? And yet, when Nash wasn't here, the cottage didn't feel quite right.

As she sipped her wine, savoring the rich, fruity notes, her gaze wandered to Nash's strong, capable fingers wrapped around his glass. A flutter of something unfamiliar stirred within, her heart suddenly pounding. Their eyes met, and in that moment, she saw a depth of emotion mirrored in his intense blue stare that both thrilled and terrified her. She set her glass down with a start.

Was she falling for this man? The exact thing she'd told her sister she was *not* doing? That he was simply the contractor she'd hired. Her thoughts tumbled around in her mind.

"You okay?" His eyes filled with concern. "You look… worried? Confused?"

She swallowed hard, her throat suddenly dry. "No, I'm fine." But even as the words left her lips, she knew they sounded hollow.

"You sure?" he murmured, his thumb slowly tracing the curve of her jawline. "You feel it too, don't you?"

She didn't even try to pretend she didn't know what he was talking about. "I feel it," she whispered.

A slight smile tilted his lips. "Ah, good. I was hoping it wasn't just me." He pushed back a lock of her hair, his fingers trailing across her flushed cheek.

"You know what I want?" He cocked an eyebrow.

"What?" She held her breath.

"I would very much like to kiss you."

Her heart raced as Nash's words hung in the air between them. Had he really just asked to kiss her? She held her breath, scarcely daring to believe it. When he leaned in and his lips met hers, a spark of electricity shot through her. Her hand, with a mind of its own, found its way to the nape of his neck as she melted into his embrace. He deepened the kiss and all rational thought fluttered away, disappearing into the night sky.

He finally pulled back and touched her cheek again. "That was nice," he murmured, his voice low and intimate.

She could only nod, her mind still reeling from the intensity of the moment. She had never felt this way before, and the realization that she was falling for this man—her contractor, no less—left her both exhilarated and terrified.

Nash's gaze held hers, and she saw the same mix of emotions reflected in his eyes. "You intrigue me, Jenna," he said, his fingers tracing the outline of her face. "Everything about you – the way you work so hard, your love for this old cottage, and your determination to restore it." He paused, his expression softening. "And..." He let out a long breath and leaned back slightly. "I'm sorry. This is too much, too fast, isn't it?"

Was it? Too much? Too fast?

"I don't want to scare you off." He searched her face.

"I don't scare easily," she managed to say.

His face lit up with an impish grin. "Well, okay then. Wanna try another kiss?"

"I sure do." She smiled up at him and he kissed her again.

He pulled her close, his arm draped around her shoulder like it belonged there. In that moment, the universe seemed to pause, leaving only the two of them wrapped together in their own little world. They remained like that for a long time, talking, kissing, laughing.

He finally looked at his watch. "I should go. It's after midnight."

"Do you turn back into a pumpkin at midnight?" she teased.

"I turn into a tired worker if I don't get my beauty sleep." He grinned, then stood and reached down a hand to help her to her feet.

She led him to the door, savoring their last few moments together. He kissed her one more time, wrapping her close in a hug before letting her go. "Good night," he said, with one last brush of his thumb along her jawline. He turned and trotted down the steps, waving once as he climbed into his truck.

She stood in the doorway long after he pulled away. She hugged her arms around herself, acutely missing his presence. This was not the night she'd been expecting. This was so, so much more.

Nash pulled his truck into his drive and turned off the motor. Yet he sat there, not moving, his mind reeling from the unexpected turn the night had taken. He ran his fingers through his hair, shoving it back, as the events of the night played over and over in his mind.

Jenna had been such a welcome surprise in his life, entering it when he least expected it. He hadn't been looking for anyone special, content with his daily routine and the familiarity of his life. But then, seemingly out of nowhere, she was just here, a light that swept through his world.

Her teasing and laughter never failed to bring a smile to his face, lighting up even the most ordinary moments. And when she looked at him with those mesmerizing chestnut-brown eyes, he swore she made it hard to breathe.

He shook his head. Here he was, acting like an infatuated schoolboy.

But sitting in the darkness of his truck, he marveled at the unexpected path his life had taken since Jenna's arrival. She had a way of making even the simplest things feel extraordinary, her presence alone enough to brighten his days and fill his thoughts.

As he finally stepped out of the vehicle and

made his way toward his house, Nash knew that tonight was a turning point. What had started as a casual friendship had become something more, something that made his heart race and his mind wander to possibilities he hadn't dared to consider for a long time. And for once, he welcomed the change with open arms.

In Jenna, he found a woman who was unapologetically herself, without any pretenses or hidden agendas. Her authenticity drew him in, made him feel at ease in her presence. Her determination was a trait he admired, as it showed her strong sense of self and unfaltering commitment to her goals.

And she'd been honest and open with him. She'd admitted she'd come here for a fresh start, even if he wasn't exactly sure why she needed that new beginning. She'd been honest about how much money she wanted to spend on the house and she'd stuck with that budget. It was refreshing to have that, honestly. He respected her for that.

His last relationship, Rhonda, had been a mess of lies—and wow, had that woman known how to spend money. Her money. His money. And Rhonda was always hiding something from him. Right up until the end—two years into the relationship—when he discovered she'd been hiding the fact she was dating someone else.

But with Jenna, he felt like what he saw in her was the real deal. She wasn't hiding anything. She was just herself with him. And he liked that. She was determined... okay, almost to the point of stubborn... but she knew what she wanted. He liked that too.

What didn't he like about the woman?

Not one single thing, as far as he could tell.

CHAPTER 13

Nash stood on Jenna's porch steps the next morning, a wide smile lighting up his eyes. "Ah, you are real. I thought maybe I'd imagined last night."

"No, I think I'm real." Her heart skipped a beat at the mere sight of him. "Come in."

He stepped inside, closed the door behind him, and turned to her. "I don't suppose I could start my day with a good morning kiss?"

"Thought you'd never ask." She stood on tiptoe and kissed him. He wrapped his arms around her and pulled her close. When they finally broke apart, he stood there grinning at her.

"Now that's a great way to start a day. I was

in such a hurry to get here that I didn't even stop at Coastal Coffee for my breakfast."

She laughed and took his hand, his skin warm against hers. "Come to the kitchen. I'll get you some coffee." She poured them both steaming mugs of coffee and handed him one. He leaned against the counter, took both mugs, and set them down before pulling her close again.

She peeked out the window over his shoulder. "What if one of your workers sees us?"

"What if they do? I don't care." He paused, his forehead wrinkling. "Do you?"

She laughed. "No, it's pretty much been years since I've worried about what people think about me or think about what I do." She was critical enough of her choices. She didn't need others judging her.

"So I should probably kiss you again," Nash said, his eyes twinkling with mischief.

"You should." She smiled as his lips settled on hers.

Her phone rang, shattering the moment, and she reluctantly pulled back, glancing over to where it sat on the counter. The photo of Marly popped onto the screen. "I should probably get that. It's my sister."

Nash nodded but didn't totally let her go, his arms still loosely encircling her waist. She grinned and spun around in his embrace to grab her phone, enjoying the playful moment despite the interruption.

"Hey, sis." Marly's voice came through, her eyes filling with concern as the video connected. "You okay? You looked a bit flushed."

Shoot. What was she thinking? It was a video call. Marly would see everything—her tousled hair, flushed cheeks, and Nash's arms around her.

"I... uh..." She tried to subtly wiggle out of Nash's arms. Her cheeks grew warm as Marly's eyes widened with interest. She hadn't planned on introducing Nash to her sister like this, caught off guard in her kitchen. This was not how she wanted her sister to find out about Nash and whatever it was that was developing between them.

"Oh, wait. There's someone there with you. Turn the phone. Hey, hello there. I'm Marly. Jenna's sister. And you are?"

"I'm Nash, ma'am." His polite response only seemed to intrigue her sister more.

"Ma'am. He has good manners. Nash, huh?" Marly broke into a wide, knowing grin that made Jenna want to end the call immediately.

"He's here working on the house. The contractor I told you about."

Nash looked at her curiously, as if expecting more of an explanation from her.

"And he's... my friend."

"Friend, huh?" Marly's brows rose skeptically. "If you say so."

"I should get to work. I'll leave you two to chat. Nice to meet you, Marly." Nash released her and headed out the door, leaving her alone to face her sister's inquisition.

Jenna sighed inwardly, knowing there was no point in trying to hide anything from her sister. Marly had always been able to read her like an open book, even from thousands of miles away.

"Spill it. What aren't you telling me?"

"Okay, we might be a tiny bit more than friends now," she admitted, feeling a flutter in her stomach as she said the words out loud.

Marly's eyes lit up with excitement. "I knew it. I just knew it. Tell me everything."

"There's not much to tell." Well, there was,

but she wasn't going to spill everything to her sister, not before she figured out things herself.

Her sister wasn't ready to let her off the hook so easily. "Do you like him? Have you gone on a date? Has he kissed you?" Marly fired off questions in rapid succession.

"Yes, yes, yes."

"A-ha. I knew it. Look at you with a boyfriend and you've only been there a few weeks," Marly teased, her smile widening.

"I admit. It was unexpected."

"Well, good for you. I'm happy for you. Now I don't have to worry about you being all alone there on the island," Marly said, her tone softening with genuine care.

"Pretty sure I wasn't ever the only one here on the island."

"You know what I mean. It's hard to move to a new place where you don't know anyone." Marly grinned again. "But, obviously, you know at least one person now. Where did you go on your date?"

"To a concert at the gazebo. Remember that big old gazebo in town? It still looks the same, though it looks freshly painted. Lots of people were there."

"So the whole town knows you had a date with Nash?"

She frowned. "Oh, they won't think it was a date, will they? They'll just think he asked me as a newcomer to town." She hadn't really considered that. Would everyone know it was a date? Small-town life was proving to be quite the adjustment.

She changed the subject from Marly's constant barrage of questions about Nash. "So what are you doing up this early?"

"Work call with someone on the East Coast. Oh, it's in five minutes. I've got to run."

"Okay, talk to you later."

"You bet you will. I'll need more details." With that, the screen went dark.

She slowly turned and looked out the window. Nash was perched on a ladder, fixing the trim on a window. His t-shirt stretched across his broad shoulders and his tool belt was slung low on his hips. She found herself unable to look away. As if he could feel her staring at him, he turned and grinned at her. She blushed, thankful he couldn't see it from that distance. She gave him a small wave and deliberately turned around. She couldn't just stand there at the window staring at him all day, now could she?

She went to the back bedroom and continued painting, stopping only for their usual mid-morning coffee break. As she worked, her thoughts kept drifting back to Nash and the unexpected turn her life had taken since she'd arrived.

Early that afternoon, Nash came inside to find her. "Got to knock off a bit early today. Headed to the mainland for dinner."

She ignored the disappointment that skittered through her. She'd hoped they could spend time together this evening, maybe a meal or a walk on the beach if her ankle would cooperate. She pushed her feelings aside, not wanting him to sense her disappointment.

"My sister bribed me with a home-cooked meal if I come fix her back door. The door is sticking, and the lock is hard to open. She says having a handyman in the family is almost as good as having a doctor or a lawyer." He flashed a grin. "And I get a nice meal out of it, so it's a good trade."

"Hope you have a good time."

"I'm sure I will. My nephews are always a

hoot to be around. Constant energy. Oh, and I have to work on another job site tomorrow. I'll miss being here and having our coffee break."

Her heart sank a little further. No time together this evening and he wouldn't be here tomorrow. She walked him to the door. He gave her a quick kiss, then seemed to think better of it. He grinned and pulled her into his arms for a longer one that left her breathless. "There. That will have to tide me over."

After Nash left, she wandered around aimlessly for a bit before deciding to just make a sandwich for dinner. After making her meal, she carried it out to the living room and sat on the couch. The wooden box called to her, and she set her plate on the coffee table. Opening the box, she pulled out the unread letters and opened the first one. She still felt a bit of guilt for reading them, but her curiosity and the possibility of finding out who these star-crossed lovers were intrigued her.

Carefully unfolding the crinkled page—it looked like it had been read over and over—she perused the words. Then she read the next one, and the next. She was starting to believe the letter writer was a man. Just a feeling she had.

At least in her mind, it was a he. She was happy to see in one letter he mentioned how great it was to see her again, but now he missed her more than ever. So they'd at least reconnected once. Was that the only time?

Between bites of her sandwich, she continued reading until there was only one letter left. She frowned when she saw the handwriting was different on this one. A different penmanship. A bit more flowery with fancy loops.

She carefully unfolded the page, though it was not as worn as the other letters. She ran her gaze down the page.

My darling,

I'm not sure how I'm going to send this or if I'm going to get any letters from you ever again. I feel sorry that our using Milton to be our go-between on our letters has caused trouble for him. Some young kids were playing in the lighthouse when they weren't supposed to. They found a letter. Thankfully, they don't know you wrote it or that it was for me. But questions are flying around town.

Milton refuses to say a word, and the town is a bit

up in arms. I fear that he might lose his job. There's talk of replacing him as the lighthouse keeper.

I'm not sure of any other way to receive your letters without anyone finding out. I believe this is a sign that we should take a break from our correspondence, though I will miss not hearing from you. I have lived for your letters and brief glimpses of your life. I will try to mail this last letter when I next get to the mainland.

Just know that I love you. Goodbye, my darling.

Yours forever

Jenna read the words again and could almost feel the pain emanating from the page. It looked like she had never gotten a chance to send the letter. Did he wonder what had happened? Did he ever find out?

As she pieced together the fragments of this star-crossed romance, Jenna felt increasingly certain that the box contained correspondence from a man, while this particular letter was penned by a woman. The absence of dates on any of the letters left her guessing, unable to know how long the relationship had gone on.

She didn't have many clues from the letters. The man did mention walking the beach in his letters, so he must have lived near the sea. And there was the one clue about Milton, the lighthouse keeper.

Tomorrow she'd go visit Dale and ask if he knew about past lighthouse keepers. Maybe that would give her some idea of where to look next to unravel this mystery.

Nash pulled into his sister's drive, his truck barely coming to a stop before his nephews came racing over. "Uncle Nash! You're here. Can you play catch with us? Please?"

He slid out of his truck. "Just for a few minutes. I need to fix your mom's door."

"Yeah, Lucas busted it."

"I did not."

"Did, too."

"Knock it off, boys," his sister, Pam, called from the doorway.

"Few minutes of catch, then I'll be in to look at your door." He tossed the ball to the boys, and the game was accompanied by shouts and laughter. It was more roughhousing than actual catch, but he thoroughly enjoyed himself.

"Okay, I'm out. I'm headed inside now. Want to get the door fixed before dinner."

"Mom made your favorite. Meatloaf and green beans. I don't know why you like green beans. They're yucky."

"She made peach pie, too."

"She's the best sister ever," he said as he headed inside. He went to work on her door, adjusting the lock repeatedly until the door would open, close, and lock easily. Then he washed up at the kitchen sink. "All fixed."

"Thanks. I'm sure it's from those boys slamming in and out all the time. I appreciate it though. Last night I spent ten minutes trying to get it locked, and then I wasn't sure I'd be able to open it again."

"You're all set now." He wandered over to where the fresh beans were simmering on the stove, smothered with a generous helping of onion and bacon. "Yum."

"If only you could teach the boys to like them. Or any vegetable, for that matter." Pam pulled the meatloaf out of the oven. "Gotta let it set for just a bit."

"Can I help with anything?"

"Nope, just pour yourself something to drink. I have fresh tea or lemonade."

He poured himself a tall glass of iced tea

and leaned against the counter while Pam finished up getting dinner ready.

"So what's new with you?" Pam's eyes twinkled and she tried to hide a grin.

"Not much," he answered noncommittally.

"That's not what I heard. I heard you've been dating someone."

He rolled his eyes. "Where'd you hear that?"

"From Mom. She says everyone on the island is talking about it." Pam grinned. "I'm supposed to get the scoop from you and let her know."

He let out a long sigh. "I only went to a concert at the gazebo."

"So you're not dating?"

"Well, I wouldn't say that either," he admitted reluctantly.

"Spill it." Her eyes lit up in triumph.

Nash set his glass down, knowing his sister wouldn't let this go. "I... I like her. Jenna. That's her name. She bought the old Weston place, and I'm helping her fix it up. She's talented and hardworking. Strict about keeping to her budget. And she's... well, she's one of those what-you-see-is-what-you-get-people. Honest."

Pam cocked her head and nodded knowingly. "You mean nothing like Rhonda?"

"Nothing. I can't take someone who hides things from me or just spends money right and left."

"And Rhonda spent your money too." Her words were laced with protective, sisterly concern.

"There was that." He smiled wryly. "But the keeping things from me, the lies. That is what finally did us in."

"Good riddance, I say. Never did like her."

"So I heard. Many times."

"When do I get to meet this new woman?"

"I'm not sure she's quite ready to meet the family. You guys are... a lot."

Feigning innocence, she raised her eyebrows. "Us?"

"Yes, you. All of you. Give me some time to get to know her better."

"But you like her, don't you?"

He nodded slowly. "I do."

His nephews burst into the kitchen and all talk of his dating life ended as chaos ensued with a fun, rowdy family dinner.

Pam walked him to the door at the end of the evening. "I'm happy for you, Nash. I thought after Rhonda... well, I thought you might be off dating for good."

"We'll have to see where this goes, Pam. Don't marry me off just yet."

She laughed and punched his arm playfully. "Okay. I'll let you at least have a second date before we plan the wedding."

He chuckled as he headed out to his truck.

CHAPTER 14

The next morning Jenna was up early, acutely aware of how quiet the house was with no workers around. She poured her coffee and went out on the deck, looking to escape the silence.

As she gazed out at the endless expanse of water, the rhythmic crashing of waves provided a soothing backdrop to her thoughts. Jenna chided herself silently. She'd spent years on her own, navigating life single-handedly. And she'd been fine. Perfectly fine. There was no reason to suddenly feel so vulnerable and dependent. She took a sip of coffee, its warmth spreading through her chest, and resolved to shake off these unexpected feelings.

A pair of pelicans flew overhead, their wings

flapping in perfect harmony as if they belonged together. She set her coffee mug on the railing and cut across the sand, pausing at the water's edge. She let the frothy foam of the waves lap at her feet. The pink hues of the morning sky stretched before her and she sucked in a deep breath of the salty air. A person could get used to mornings like this.

She finally turned around and went back to the cottage, her mind racing with things she wanted to get done today, wondering what time Second Finds opened so she could talk to Dale. Maybe she'd drop by Coastal Coffee and have some breakfast first. She glanced at her watch, certain she'd missed Nash by now. Beverly said Nash was always her first customer, and she'd been open for over an hour by now.

She debated on driving or walking, but decided her ankle still wasn't up for that long of a walk. She drove to Coastal Coffee and parked near the entrance. As she walked inside, Beverly and Maxine motioned her back to the counter. She threaded her way through the tables and slipped onto a stool at the counter.

"Well, look who's here. I do believe it is Nash's date to the concert," Beverly teased.

"Yes, I'm certain you're right." Maxine agreed with a smile.

"Good morning," she said, ignoring their teasing. And it just proved Marly's point that the whole town would know she was dating Nash now.

"Nash was in this morning but just smiled at me when I asked if you two had been out on another date after the concert."

"That's the only one." She glanced up at the chalkboard over the counter. "I think I'll have a cinnamon roll today. And coffee." She hoped that would change the subject.

Beverly poured her a cup of coffee. "Bet he asks you out again soon."

Just then, Miss Eleanor walked up to them. "Good morning." She nodded at them. "Jenna, did you enjoy the concert at the gazebo?"

Did everyone in town know she was there? "I did."

"Good. That Nash is a nice young man."

She tried again to change the subject. "I'm headed over to Second Finds after breakfast. Found a few clues in the letters I found hidden in my cottage."

Miss Eleanor frowned. "You found hidden letters in the old Weston place?"

"I did. And a photograph of a couple."

"Dale mentioned that you came by and showed him the photograph you found. He's been looking into it," Maxine said.

"If the letters were hidden, don't you think that meant they were private?" Miss Eleanor raised an eyebrow and sent her a disapproving look.

A look that immediately brought back her feelings of guilt for reading the letters. "I... I was hoping to figure out who wrote them and maybe give them back to their families. I'd think at the very least the family would appreciate the photo being returned."

"Some things are better left in the past. And some things should remain private." Miss Eleanor's words were more a command than a comment. With a dismissive nod, she turned and headed to her regular table.

"I better go get her fresh cream for her coffee." Maxine hurried into the kitchen.

Beverly leaned close. "Don't worry about Miss Eleanor. She has... opinions. About almost everything. And she's very protective about the island's history."

"Maybe she's right. Maybe I should have left the letters unopened."

"Or maybe the family will be very grateful to have the photograph you found if the letters help you figure out who they are."

Dale's face lit up with a warm smile as Jenna stepped into Second Finds. The shop's familiar scent of old books and polished wood surrounded her, a comforting welcome after the tension at the coffee shop with Miss Eleanor.

"Jenna, there you are. Glad you came by. I've been trying to figure out who the people are in the photograph. Not having much luck. But I did come up with a little hint."

"Oh?" Her curiosity was aroused.

"I do think in looking at the background, it was taken near the ferry landing. There's a corner of a building in the photo and I think it might be the old building that used to be there."

"Really?"

"Yes, and the strange thing is that the painting Beverly found had a building just like it, only it wasn't exactly ours. Though maybe the painter just took some liberties with it and it was ours."

"I read some more of the letters from the box."

"Did you find out anything?"

"I'm afraid I didn't find out much. But one of the letters was written in different handwriting. I think it was a woman's penmanship. And she mentioned a Milton in the letter. Said he was the lighthouse keeper. I think he was the go-between for them. She mentioned he might lose his job because a letter was found by some kids and he wouldn't say anything about it. The town started to distrust him because of his silence."

"I do have some books and papers on the history of the lighthouse. Let's go take a look at them."

She followed Dale into a backroom filled with boxes and books. "I know it looks like a mess, but I do have a system." Dale laughed as he headed over to a shelf and pulled out a box, setting it on a large wooden table that dominated the center of the room. "There are records of the ships coming in and going out. Major storms. And somewhere, I'm certain there was a list of the lighthouse keepers."

They both grabbed some papers from the box and started going through them, carefully examining each document for any clues. After an hour of meticulous searching, neither of them had found anything substantial. Dale frowned, his brow creasing in concentration. "Let me check one more box. I have a feeling we might be overlooking something."

He brought another battered box to the table, its corners worn and edges battered from years of storage. Reaching in, he pulled out an old book with yellowed pages and falling apart at the binding. He opened it gently, and a smile spread across his face. "This is what I remember. It's notes from the lighthouse keepers. There are newer books in the box too, but this one is from the nineteen twenties. It might give us a clue."

She stood and peeked over his shoulder. He ran his finger down the page, then turned and looked at the next page. After a few pages, he paused and tapped his finger on the weathered page. "There. There it is. Milton Carlisle."

"Carlisle." Surprise colored her tone. "As in Nash Carlisle?"

"I would guess so. Their family has been here on the island for a long time."

That was not what she wanted to hear. Not someone from Nash's family. She was not going to go looking into his family's past. What if she found out something that they didn't want to know? Something that was better kept a secret. It was one thing to think about trying to solve the mystery when it was strangers. But if it involved Nash's family?

What if she discovered some long-kept secret? Or worse, what if she only scratched the surface, leaving half-truths and misunderstandings in her wake? She couldn't risk repeating past mistakes because she didn't do enough research. What if it happened again?

Where was her resolve to never investigate someone ever again? Had she not learned her lesson?

She turned to Dale, forcing a smile. "I really appreciate your help."

"I'll still keep looking into the photo for you."

"Ah... I'm beginning to think that's not a good idea. Maybe Miss Eleanor was right, and some things are just meant to remain in the past."

"Maybe. But I find the history of Magnolia Key absolutely fascinating." Dale set the worn book gently on the table. "If you change your mind and want to do more research, just let me know. I'm always happy to help."

She managed a weak smile before leaving Dale poring over the old papers. She stepped outside onto the sidewalk as the sun beat down on her, throwing a spotlight on her choices.

Well, here's a choice she could make. She could abandon this whole investigation. She never should have opened those letters and read them. It had all been a mistake from the very start. There was no way she was going poking into Nash's family.

CHAPTER 15

Nash arrived at Jenna's cottage early the next morning, eager to see her. He'd missed her yesterday. Seeing her. Kissing her. Watching her eyes light up with laughter. When she opened the door, he immediately noticed the absence of her usual warm, welcoming smile. Concern washed over him as he stepped inside, his eyes searching her face for any sign of what might be troubling her. "You okay?" he asked gently, his voice laced with worry.

"What? Sure. I just didn't sleep well last night."

Her response was quick, almost dismissive. She avoided his gaze and a pang of unease flickered through him. Something was definitely off, but he didn't want to push her if she wasn't ready to talk about it. "I'm sorry. Something keeping you awake?"

She still avoided his gaze. "No, not really. Just restless." Without further explanation, she headed to the kitchen, leaving him to follow along behind, his mind racing with possibilities.

Determined to lighten the mood and bring a smile to her face, Nash tossed her a playful grin. "So, do I get a good morning kiss?" he asked, hoping to break through the tension that seemed to hang in the air.

To his relief, she stopped and turned to him, giving him a quick kiss before turning back to the coffeemaker, pouring a mug, and handing it to him.

"You not having any?"

"I've already had more than enough." Her voice sounded strained. "I better get to work on the guest bedroom. I'd really like to get it finished so Dale can deliver the dresser."

He narrowed his eyes, carefully scanning her expression. Something was off. He knew it. And that kiss? It had barely qualified as a kiss at all, just a brief brush of her lips against his. But perhaps she was being truthful. Maybe she really was just exhausted from a restless night.

"Alright, I'll let you get to your project, then," he said, trying to push aside his concerns.

She nodded, offering him a faint smile before vanishing down the hallway. He carried the steaming mug of coffee outside, the warmth seeping into his hands as he checked on the progress of his crew. Satisfied with their work, he set about finishing the trim on another window, the repetitive motions allowing his mind to wander.

He glanced at his watch and frowned, realizing Jenna hadn't called him in for their mid-morning coffee. Maybe she wasn't at a breaking point in her work—and she had said she wanted to get the guest room finished. Still, he couldn't shake the nagging feeling that something was wrong. He tried to concentrate on his task, but his thoughts kept drifting back to Jenna. Was she truly just tired, or was it something more?

He finally couldn't take it any longer and went inside to check on her. He paused in the doorway to the guest room. "Hey, it's looking great. Looks like you're almost finished."

She straightened up, pressing her hand to the small of her back. "Almost."

"You want to take a break and go grab some

lunch somewhere?" He smiled at her, hoping to coax a smile from her in return, but no luck.

"I think I'll just keep working." She avoided his gaze.

He stepped into the room and walked over to her, taking her hand. "Are you sure you're okay? Is something wrong?"

"No, I already told you. I'm just tired." She looked away.

"Okay. If you're sure that's all it is." He brushed back a lock of her hair, his fingertips grazing her cheeks.

She stepped back. "I should get back to it."

"Right. I should too." He turned and walked out of the room, frowning. Had he done something to upset her? Or maybe she'd changed her mind about them?

Something was wrong. He was sure of it. The distance in her eyes. The way she'd pulled away from his touch. He was certain she was keeping something from him.

Jenna set down the paint roller after Nash left the room, a heavy sigh escaping her lips. The weight of her secret bore down on her, making it difficult to act naturally around him. How could she possibly kiss him or be close to him while keeping the secret about the lighthouse keeper? It felt wrong, dishonest even. It had ruined their budding intimacy.

She wished they'd never even found the old wooden box. That it had remained hidden. And maybe this was all for the best, anyway. After all, she had no business diving into another investigation, not after the promises she'd made to herself. What had possessed her to start reading those letters in the first place? She silently chastised herself for her momentary lapse in judgment.

She'd made a promise to herself that her investigative days were over. She promised herself anew that she'd keep that vow.

With renewed determination, she picked up the paint roller, attacking the walls with an eye on completion. She focused on the task at hand, pouring her energy into finishing the room, eager to move on to refinishing the bookshelves. The sooner she completed these projects, the sooner she could unpack more of her belongings, surrounding herself with familiar comforts. She longed to banish the sea of boxes that mocked her, to make the cottage finally feel like a true home.

As she worked, carefully covering the last wall, she reaffirmed her vow to leave her investigative days behind, to resist the temptation of unraveling the mysteries that lurked within the old letters. She had come to Magnolia Key for a fresh start, to escape the ghosts of her past, and she refused to let her curiosity jeopardize the new life she was building for herself.

Late that afternoon, Jenna set the paint roller down in the tray, surveying the freshly painted walls with a sense of satisfaction. The cheerful color had transformed the guest room, bringing it to life just as she'd envisioned. The afternoon sun cast a warm glow through the window, highlighting the new hue and making the space feel even more inviting.

Nash's sudden appearance at the doorway startled her. "Looks like you're almost finished."

"Almost," she confirmed, wiping her hands on a towel tucked into her pocket.

"You want to go out and grab a quick dinner? You look too tired to cook." His voice held a touch of concern.

Jenna hesitated, a twinge of guilt nagging at

her conscience. She knew the way she was acting today was putting a strain on their relationship, but she couldn't bring herself to fully embrace their connection while keeping secrets from him. "I… ah… I think I'll just grab a sandwich or something," she replied, avoiding his gaze.

A flicker of disappointment showed clearly on his features. "Okay. Well, I hope you get a good night's sleep." He turned and walked away without even trying to kiss her, leaving her alone in the freshly painted room.

Not that she blamed him. She'd certainly been distant with him. But she firmly believed it was for his own good. He didn't need to know his family was involved in this mystery in some way. And she didn't need to be investigating anyone or anything, either.

She gathered her painting supplies and began cleaning up, her mind still grappling with the conflicting emotions that swirled within her. If only she could find a way to navigate her growing feelings for Nash while keeping her past and her promises to herself intact.

CHAPTER 16

Nash arrived at Jenna's the next morning with a sense of optimism filling him. He hoped that after a good night's sleep, the tension between them would fade, and they could return to their easy-going friendship... and more. However, as he stepped inside, the same awkward atmosphere from the previous day greeted him.

Determined to address the issue head-on, Nash turned to face Jenna. His eyes sought hers, searching for answers. "What's going on? Things have changed between us. At least on your end. My feelings for you are the same." He paused, gathering his courage. In a moment of raw honesty, he laid his cards on the table, exposing his feelings to her. "I care about you,

Jenna. And I thought we were growing closer. But now, it feels like you're pulling away. Please, talk to me. Help understand what's going on."

"I think... maybe we rushed into things. I mean, we hardly know each other." She still wouldn't meet his eyes. "There is just so much going on in my life right now. This move. Getting the cottage fixed up. It's all... it's a lot. I need... I need space."

Nash studied her face, searching for clues, but she kept her gaze averted. The distance between them felt like a chasm, and he struggled to bridge the gap. "I understand that you're going through a lot right now, with the move and the cottage renovations," he said, choosing his words carefully. "But I thought we were in this together, that there was something special between us." Just a few days ago, he would have sworn she felt the same way.

He paused, giving her a chance to respond, but she remained silent. The uncertainty gnawed at him, and he wondered if there was more to her sudden change of heart than just the stress of her new life. "If you need some space, I'll respect that," he continued, unable to keep the tinge of disappointment out of his voice. "I do care about you, and I want to support you in whatever way you need."

As the words left his mouth, a dull ache settled in his chest. He'd thought they were growing closer, that their connection was deepening. But now, faced with her withdrawal, he questioned everything. Was she simply overwhelmed by the changes in her life, or was she trying to let him down gently? The thought sent a chill through him, and he silently cursed his inexperience with relationships.

He wanted to reach out to her, to pull her into his arms and reassure her that they could face anything together. But he held back, knowing that he had to honor her request for space, no matter how much it pained him. "Just know that I'm here for you, whenever you're ready," he said softly, his eyes searching hers for any sign of the connection they had shared.

As the silence stretched between them, he felt a growing sense of unease. He'd laid his heart on the line, but now he wondered if he had misread the situation entirely. The doubts crept in, whispering that perhaps he had been foolish to believe that someone like Jenna could ever truly care for him. What he'd believed was happening between them, their connection, seemed to slip through his fingers.

A pain stabbed in his chest, and he was certain she wasn't telling him everything. But he needed to give her what she wanted, what she needed. "If space is what you need, that's what I'll give you."

"I think it's for the best. For both of us." She turned and took a few steps away from him, facing the wall between the kitchen and the living room. She flung out her arm. "I was thinking maybe we should take out this wall like you suggested. It would really open up the space."

Her abrupt change of topic, along with what she said, surprised him. "I thought you said it wouldn't be in your budget?"

She shrugged, a gesture of dismissal. "It's only money."

Nash studied her closely, trying to discern the emotions hidden beneath her nonchalant exterior. "So you really want to tear down this wall?"

"Yes, I think I do." She nodded slowly, her gaze fixed on the wall as if it held the answers to everything.

"Okay, whatever you say," he said as the

unease grew inside him. As he turned and walked outside, doubts mounted inside of him. He knew she was keeping something from him. He could see it in the shadows that flickered in her eyes, in the way she avoided his gaze.

And the last thing he wanted was a woman keeping secrets from him. He'd been down that road before, and the scars it left still ached deep within him. The thought of history repeating itself filled him with a sense of dread, a cold weight settling in the pit of his stomach. He drew in a deep breath, the salty sea air filling his lungs, but it did little to ease the tightness in his chest.

Yes, the last thing he needed right now—or ever—was a woman keeping secrets from him.

Jenna groaned inwardly, mentally kicking herself for her impulsive declaration about tearing down the wall. What had she been thinking? It was just the first thing that had popped into her mind. It was a spur-of-the-moment idea, a desperate attempt to change the subject and divert Nash's attention from the emotions she was trying so hard to conceal. And the secret about his family she was hiding. But now, faced with the reality of her budget, she realized the folly of her words.

She was a meticulous planner, always careful with her finances, and the thought of taking on such a significant expense without proper consideration made her stomach churn. To afford the wall removal, she would have to make sacrifices elsewhere, cutting back on other aspects of the renovation that she had so carefully mapped out.

As if the universe had a twisted sense of humor, her phone rang at that precise moment, Marly's smiling face illuminating the screen. Jenna hesitated, her finger hovering over the answer button. She wasn't sure if she had the energy to face her sister's inevitable barrage of questions, to put on a brave face and pretend that everything was fine when her world felt like it was unraveling at the seams.

With a heavy sigh, she resigned herself to the conversation and tapped the green button. "Hey, sis. What's up?" she greeted, trying to inject a note of cheerfulness into her voice.

"Not much. Just thought I'd check on you." Marly's bubbly response filled the quiet of her cottage. "What's up with you?"

She didn't really want to talk about her strained relationship with Nash and the mounting pressures of the cottage remodel. And she didn't want to burden her sister with her troubles. She simply answered. "Same here. Same old, same old." *You know, except that I ruined things with Nash and I'm overspending on the cottage.*

"How's Nash?"

"He's fine," Jenna replied, the words tumbling out a little too quickly, a little too automatically. She cringed, knowing that her sister's keen intuition would likely pick up on the underlying tension in her voice. But for now, she clung to the pretense, hoping to push the conversation in a different direction.

Marly's eyes narrowed as she studied her sister through the screen. "How fine? You two have another date planned yet?"

She hesitated and turned her face from the screen. "No, I don't think we're going to."

"What? Why not? I thought you liked him."

"I do, but…" She sighed. "I just don't think it's a good idea."

Marly's brow creased in confusion. "Hold on. How did you get from you like him to you don't think you should date him?"

"It's complicated," she offered weakly.

"I've got time to listen to your excuses—I mean, your complications." Marly's tone was light, but Jenna could hear the concern underneath.

Knowing her sister wouldn't let it go, Jenna sank onto the couch, her shoulders slumping. "So, I read some more letters. Found out about this lighthouse keeper who is involved in the whole mystery. And in…" She paused, catching herself before she said 'investigating.' That wasn't her life anymore. "In looking into things, I found out it's someone related to Nash."

"Was he surprised?" Marly asked, leaning closer to the screen.

"Uh… no."

Marly's frown deepened. "He wasn't?"

"No… because I didn't tell him." Jenna's voice grew quieter. "And I'm not looking into things anymore. It's not my place. I put the letters and the photo back in the box. I'm done with it."

Her sister's expression softened, understanding dawning in her eyes. "Because of what happened back in San Francisco? You know this isn't the same, sis."

Her throat tightened. "Isn't it? What if I uncover something that shouldn't be uncovered?

Or worse, what if I only find out the partial truth again?" Her voice cracked. "I cannot ruin anyone else's life. I can't."

"I get it. Why you feel that way. But maybe you should just tell him the truth. Let him decide if he wants to look into things or not."

"I think it's smarter if I just drop the whole thing."

"I don't." Marly shook her head. "I think you should deal with it head-on."

"I can't. I've already kept it a secret. And if I tell him now, I'd have to explain why I kept it a secret. And I'm not ready to… to explain things. What I did."

"Jenna, I wish you'd forgive yourself. Let it go."

"I take full responsibility for my actions. What happened because of my choices." She held up a hand, her voice firm. "And we're not going to talk about this any longer. Please, Marly, just give it a rest."

"Okay, but now I'll have to go back to worrying about you." Marly gave her a small smile.

"Or not. You could just let me live my life." The words came out harsher than she'd intended.

"Fine. I hear you loud and clear. I should go anyway. Bye, Jenna." And with that, Marly ended the call before Jenna could even attempt to apologize.

She sat there, feeling the weight of her words and the strain on her relationship with her sister. She was making an even bigger mess of her life. How had moving to the peaceful island of Magnolia Key ended up... like this?

CHAPTER 17

The last thing Nash wanted tonight was a family dinner. Everyone asking questions. But he couldn't disappoint his mother. The dinner had been planned for weeks. Family gatherings had become increasingly rare, with everyone's busy schedules making it a challenge to coordinate a time when they could all be together.

He walked over to his parent's house—it was only about five minutes from his—and climbed the porch steps, steeling himself for the inevitable questions. His family didn't disappoint.

He had barely crossed the threshold when his sister approached him, a beer in hand and a playful glint in her eye. "You know, Nash, I've been thinking," she said, handing him the cold bottle. "You really should have invited Jenna to join you tonight. We're all dying to meet her."

"Drop it, will you?"

Pam's eyes narrowed at his sharp tone. "You okay?"

"I'm fine." He softened his tone but hoped to put an end to the conversation.

His mother came into the room. "I should have insisted you bring Jenna with you," she said, echoing Pam's words. "We'd love to meet her."

Pam snickered.

He took a swig of his beer, silently wishing he could escape the scrutiny and enjoy a moment of peace without all the questions. He felt a twinge of guilt as he offered up the partial truth. "Ah, she was busy tonight." Not really a lie. She was busy tonight. Busy avoiding anything having to do with him.

"That's too bad. Well, dinner's not quite ready yet. The boys are playing catch with your father in the backyard. Your brothers are having a hot debate going on about some baseball player."

"Thanks, I'll go out and settle the debate." And escape the questions.

He headed out to the backyard. As soon as he stepped outside, his brother greeted him. "I hear you're dating someone."

"Not really." He kept his voice neutral.

"That's not what mom said," his other brother joined in. "She mentioned you went to some concert at the gazebo. And you're working on her house."

"I was just being friendly to someone new in town. And yes, I took the job of repairs on her cottage." Would the questions never end?

His nephews rushed over, their small hands tugging his and dragging him over to their game of catch. Which was fine with him. At least they weren't asking him about Jenna.

Soon his mom called them inside. They all gathered around the table and had a rowdy family dinner full of conversation and laughter. After dessert, Pam turned to her other brothers. "Could you take the boys outside and tire them out for me? And Mom and Dad. Why don't you go out and sit on the deck? Nash will help with the dishes, won't you?" Pam offered up his help without hesitation. But he knew what that meant. She wanted to corner him to ask more questions. Resigned to his fate, he nodded in agreement.

As everyone filed out of the dining room, their chatter and laughter fading into the evening air, Nash found himself alone with Pam. He took his time clearing the table, his movements deliberately slow and measured. Each plate and utensil seemed to take an eternity to gather, as if he could somehow delay the inevitable conversation by prolonging this simple task.

Pam watched him with a mixture of amusement and exasperation, her arms crossed over her chest as she leaned against the kitchen counter. "If you went any slower, you could just wait and clear the breakfast dishes too," she teased, her eyes rolling in mock frustration. He cracked a smile at his sister's good-natured ribbing, even as he braced himself for the impending barrage of questions

"I'm working on it." He brought in another load of dishes.

"Here, I've rinsed those. Load them in the dishwasher." She pointed to a stack of rinsed dishes.

He methodically placed them in the dishwasher, making sure the silverware was handle downward just like his mother insisted.

"You were awfully quiet at dinner." Pam

handed him another plate. "Everything okay with you?"

"Yes." He put the dish in the dishwasher and sighed. "No. Something happened between Jenna and me and I don't know what. She's... standoffish now. Says too much is going on in her life to date right now."

Pam's expression softened. "Maybe she just needs time." She offered him some hope.

"Maybe. But I swear she's hiding something from me. I can see it in her eyes. And then... she decided to add to the project even though she said tearing down the wall between the living room and kitchen was out of her budget."

"I'm sorry things aren't working out. I thought you'd finally found someone that you were at least going to try and have a relationship with."

"I was trying," he said flatly. "She no longer is."

Pam turned and looked directly at him. "And you didn't do anything, say anything to cause this?"

"No, I didn't. I swear." A hint of defensiveness crept into his voice. "I know I'm not great with women, but... it was just like overnight she changed her mind."

"Did you try talking to her? Asking her what's wrong? What's changed?"

"I did. I even…" He paused, not sure he should share this. "I… I told her I had feelings for her. But she basically ignored it." He put the last dish in the dishwasher. "I'm going to go say goodnight to Mom, then I'm going to head out."

Pam reached out and touched his arm. "I'm sorry, Nash. I really am."

"Yeah, me too." He attempted a nonchalant shrug but knew it was useless. Pam could always see right through him.

CHAPTER 18

Beverly welcomed Nash as he came in for his usual breakfast. He smiled briefly, but went and took a table without his usual morning banter. She brought him over a cup of coffee, studying him with a touch of concern. Nash was normally so chatty and upbeat. Something seemed off today.

"We've got those peach scones you like," she offered, hoping to coax a more cheerful response from him.

"Think I'll just have biscuits and gravy this morning." He reached for the mug, his gaze distant.

"Sure thing. It will be up in a sec." She turned away to greet another customer coming in, but her thoughts lingered on Nash.

When she returned with his breakfast, she set it on the table, then asked him, "How's the repair work going on Jenna's cottage? Haven't seen her in a bit. She doing okay?"

"Repairs are going fine. Hope to finish up soon." Nash's response was curt, almost evasive.

She noticed he didn't say how Jenna was doing. Come to think of it, no one had mentioned seeing Nash and Jenna together around town recently. Maybe they'd just been busy. But she couldn't shake the feeling that there was more to the story. She'd known Nash since he was a boy, and it wasn't like him to be so withdrawn.

As she moved back behind the counter, Beverly promised herself that she would keep an eye on the situation. If something had happened between Nash and Jenna, she wanted to be there to support them. In a small town like Magnolia Key, folks looked out for each other. And right now, it seemed like Nash might need a friend to lean on, whether he realized it or not.

She bustled around the coffee shop, tending to the morning rush. She refilled coffee mugs and greeted regulars. Frowning, she noticed Nash was gone. There was cash on the table for his bill. It wasn't like him to leave without saying goodbye or at least giving a friendly wave.

Just then, Jenna came into the coffee shop. She took a table near the window. Beverly hurried over with the coffeepot. "Coffee?"

"Please."

"You just missed Nash." Beverly paused and frowned. "He sure wasn't acting himself."

"Oh?" Jenna didn't look surprised.

"No, he was… quiet. A bit withdrawn." She shrugged. "Maybe he just has a lot going on right now."

"Maybe," Jenna answered, her gaze fixed on the swirling coffee in her mug.

She studied Jenna's face, noting the subtle signs of sadness around her eyes. "You too still seeing each other?"

Jenna let out a long sigh. "Just when he's there working on the cottage. We're not… dating… if that's what you're asking."

"I thought you two had really hit it off."

"I just have a lot going on right now. It's not really the right time to start dating someone."

Beverly could sense there was more to the story, but she held back from prying further. Instead, she offered a sympathetic smile. "That's too bad. I thought the two of you were a good fit, but sometimes we meet the right person at the wrong time."

She was certainly proof of that. Only... she'd thought that Cliff was the right person at the right time. *He'd* just decided it was the wrong time. Without really telling her. He'd just left her. But that was in the past, and she rarely thought about it. Usually. She pushed the thoughts away.

"You having any more luck figuring out who wrote those letters you found?"

"I... I've decided to quit looking. They must have had a good reason for hiding them. And, like I said, I'm really busy."

Jenna's gaze drifted to the chalkboard, her eyes scanning the day's specials without really seeing them. Her shoulders were tense, and her fingers fidgeted with the napkin on the table. It was clear that something was bothering her, but Beverly knew better than to push.

"I'll have the yogurt parfait and a glass of orange juice," Jenna said, finally looking up and giving her a slight smile.

"I'll bring that right out." She hurried away, sure she wasn't getting the whole story about Nash and Jenna, or the letters.

The morning rush soon swept Beverly up in

a whirlwind of orders and conversations, the cafe filling with the chatter of locals. She moved between tables with practiced ease, refilling mugs and delivering plates of steaming breakfast fare. It wasn't until the crowd began to thin that she realized Jenna had slipped away unnoticed.

Maxine walked by, balancing a tray on her hip. Beverly stopped her. "Did you see Jenna leave?"

"A bit ago," Maxine replied, nodding toward the register. "I rang her out. She seemed like she had a lot on her mind."

"Wonder what's up with her and Nash. Neither one of them seemed like themselves this morning. They sure seemed to be a bit smitten with each other. Now, even though each of them insists nothing is wrong, I'm sure there is."

"I wonder if it has something to do with Nash's uncle? Well, I think it was his something like his great-great-uncle? Maybe three greats?"

"What are you talking about?"

"Dale said that when he and Jenna were looking into those letters and that photo she found in her cottage, that they came across some information. One of the lighthouse keepers was Nash's relative."

"Really? That's interesting."

"And it appears he had something to do with the letters. The courier between the letter writers or something like that."

"That's strange, because Jenna said she wasn't looking into the letters anymore. That she was too busy."

Maxine shook her head. "Beats me."

Beverly turned to go back to work, now positive she wasn't getting the whole story. But she was going to keep an eye on Jenna and Nash. After all, she was nothing if not persistent when it came to looking out for her friends.

Jenna ran errands after breakfast, anything to keep from heading back to the cottage. She just wasn't ready to face Nash again. She wandered the aisles of the grocery store, picking up items she didn't really need, until she couldn't delay any longer. The ice cream she had impulsively bought would soon melt if she didn't get it into the freezer. She returned home and saw Nash's truck in the drive, but no sigh of him out front. Maybe she could just sneak inside with her groceries.

The coast seemed clear as she put the groceries away, peeking out the window every so often to check for any movement outside. Just as she was beginning to relax, a knock sounded at the door, shattering the temporary illusion of solitude. Steeling herself, she headed to answer it.

Nash stood there looking incredibly handsome and... distant. "Thought I'd take a look at that wall you want torn down."

She stood there awkwardly, shifting from foot to foot. Now was the time to confess. "I... I changed my mind. I think I'll leave it. After looking at the numbers again, I don't think now is a good time."

He looked at her in exasperation. "You sure about that? This is your final decision?"

"I'm sure," she said it more sharply than she'd intended. Jenna immediately regretted her tone, but the tension between them was like a solid concrete wall.

He stared at her, his blue eyes piercing and unwavering. "Fine. If that's how you want it." He paused, his jaw clenching slightly before he continued. "I need access to your circuit board. Got to throw a circuit to rewire the ceiling fan on your front porch. May I come in?"

Jenna stepped aside, feeling the frigid rift between them as he entered the cottage. The air seemed to grow colder with each step he took, and she wrapped her arms around herself, trying to ward off the chill that had settled in her bones. Nash headed back to the small storeroom where the circuit board was located, his footsteps echoing in the silence that stretched between them.

He returned moments later, his face an unreadable mask as he walked past her and out the door without saying a word. The click of the latch as the door closed behind him sounded like a final, definitive statement, and Jenna felt her heart sink.

She'd not only missed out on having a good friend here on Magnolia Key, but she'd also shut the door on any possibility of their friendship becoming something more. The realization hit her like a physical blow, and she walked over and sank down onto the couch, her head in her hands. But she was doing the right thing, she reminded herself. She would not dig into his family's past, no matter how much her curiosity gnawed at her. She'd learned that lesson the hard way, and she wouldn't make the same mistake twice.

If pushing Nash away was the only way to protect him from anyone probing into his family's history, then that's what she would do. Even if it meant sacrificing their friendship and any chance of a future together. Jenna sighed, the weight of her decision settling heavily on her shoulders as she looked around the empty cottage, feeling more alone than ever before.

CHAPTER 19

Nash tightened the last screw on the ceiling fan, securing it in place. He stepped back to admire his handiwork, but the satisfaction was short-lived as he realized he'd need to knock on Jenna's door again to re-enter her cottage and restore the electricity. The awkwardness between them gnawed at him.

And what was with her on-again, off-again decision on tearing down the wall between the living room and the kitchen? Was she just determined to keep him off balance?

He'd initially believed that Jenna was a straightforward, what-you-see-is-what-you-get kind of woman. But now, he questioned his judgment. How could he have been so wrong about her? The realization stung, and he felt like a knucklehead for allowing himself to be fooled.

He sighed, gathered his tools, and knocked on the door again. She answered without saying a word, just stepping aside for him. He went and threw the circuit and came back to the door. She was still standing there and he could have sworn for a fleeting moment he saw a sad look lingering in those brown eyes of hers. The eyes that now haunted him.

Buck up, buddy.

"Thanks. I'll get out of your way." He stepped outside and gave her one last look as she closed the door behind him. Suddenly he couldn't bear to be here, at her cottage, near her. What a chump he'd been to fall for her.

He needed to clear his head and come to terms with the fact that whatever connection he thought they had was nothing more than an illusion. As he made his way back to his truck, he couldn't shake the feeling of disappointment and regret that settled in his chest.

He decided to go grab lunch at Beverly's before the cafe closed. Anything to escape the tension he felt when he was near Jenna.

He walked into Coastal Coffee as the lunch crowd was dying down. The cool interior a welcome relief from the oppressive heat outside. He took a table and Beverly walked up, smiling. "Two times in one day."

"Guess it's your lucky day," he replied, his attempt at humor falling flat.

"So Maxine was telling me about what you found in those letters from Jenna's cottage. So your great-uncle—or was it two or three greats —was involved somehow?"

He frowned. "What are you talking about?"

"That Milton guy in the letters. The one who was the go-between. He was your relative, right? And then he lost his job because of it?"

"I have no idea what you're talking about." He narrowed his eyes.

"You don't? Maxine said that Jenna and Dale discovered his identity."

"She hasn't said a word to me." His jaw clenched, the betrayal stinging more than he cared to admit. "You know what? I've changed my mind. Not hungry." Without another word, he turned on his heel and stalked out of the coffee shop, his anger simmering just beneath the surface as he tried to make sense of this new revelation.

Questions swirled in his mind as he walked, his pace quickening with each step. Why hadn't

Jenna told him about this connection? The thought of her keeping secrets, especially ones that involved his own family history, left a bitter taste in his mouth. He needed answers, and he needed them now.

How could Jenna have kept this from him? She hadn't even mentioned a lighthouse keeper or that the man was his relative. How could she find out all this and not say a word to him? He'd been right. She'd been keeping secrets from him. But why?

Only one way to find out. He drove back to her cottage, his truck tires crushing the shells on the drive. He leapt out of the truck and, in three long strides, crossed the distance to the porch. He bounded up the stairs, hardly noticing the ceiling fan now making lazy circles above him.

He rapped on the door. Then rapped again —almost pounding. She opened the door, her eyes wide with surprise. "I thought you'd left for the day."

"I had. I'm back. I need answers."

"About what?"

"Two words. Milton Carlisle."

She flinched. "Who?"

"My great-uncle." He pinned her with a hard stare. "Don't try and pretend. You didn't even tell me? That the guy acting as the courier was my relative? Did you know I'm living in a house that used to be in his part of the family? I don't understand why you'd keep this a secret from me. I didn't even know that there was a lighthouse keeper involved in this."

His anger simmered as he struggled to understand Jenna's motives. Why did women always seem to deceive him? His jaw clenched as he fought to keep his emotions in check.

"I... found out in the last letter." Her voice was barely audible.

"So you hid all this from me? Is it too much to just tell the truth?" He shoved his hands in his pockets, trying to reel in his anger. Why did he always seem to find women who lied to him? Hid things from him. The familiar sting of betrayal pierced through him, his heart hardening in his chest. Why was he always letting women make a fool of him?

"I... I just wanted to let it all drop." Her eyes filled with uncertainty. "It wasn't mine to look into. I thought I was protecting you. Your family. Some secrets are best left in the past, like Miss Eleanor told me."

"So you decided not to tell me anything about it? To lie to me?"

She stepped back. To his surprise, her eyes filled with tears, though she valiantly tried to hold them back. "I… I'm sorry." Her voice was barely a whisper, and thick with emotion. She turned away, but not before he saw one lone tear trail down her cheek.

And just like that, his hardened heart cracked. He reached out and took her arm, stopping her. "Jenna… you're crying. I didn't mean to make you cry."

She slashed her hand across her cheek, wiping away the tear. She turned to him. "I was trying to do the right thing," she said, her voice soft and broken. "I wanted to just let it all drop. I wish we'd never found those stupid letters." Her voice splintered.

"I don't understand." He shook his head, confused at her comments. "We could have looked into this together. After all, he is my relative."

"But what if we find out something bad? Something that they tried to keep hidden? Or what… what if we only find out part of the truth?"

He frowned. "Part of it?"

"Yes, like last time."

He had to strain to even hear her. "What last time?"

"The reason I came to Magnolia. The reason I gave up investigative reporting. The reason I vowed never to get involved with investigating things again. I can't ruin anyone else's life."

Instinctively, he reached out and took her hand in his. "Jenna, talk to me," he urged softly. "Explain why you're so upset."

She lifted her gaze to meet his, and he found himself lost in the depths of her eyes, now shimmering with unshed tears. "I got assigned an investigation. It was looking into this man who was under investigation. I found evidence of fraud and he was arrested and convicted. He swore he was innocent." She looked away for a moment. "I was there in the courtroom when they read his conviction. He looked directly at me with so much pain in his eyes."

"But why was this your fault if you were just doing your job and found the proof of his guilt?"

"Because he wasn't guilty. And in my heart, I believed him when he said he was innocent. But instead of digging deeper, my boss sent me on to investigate something else. And the man went to jail for two years." Tears flowed down her cheeks now. "He missed the birth of his daughter. His first child. And the first two years of her life."

Seeing the pain etched across her features, he didn't press and waited for her to continue.

"Then new evidence was found—evidence I should have found if I'd done my investigating properly—and his conviction was overturned. But that doesn't erase the fact I took away two years of his life."

As her words hung in the air between them, Nash felt a deep ache in his chest. He wanted nothing more than to pull her into his arms and comfort her, but he held back, unsure of how she would react. "Jenna, I'm so sorry."

"Don't feel sorry for me. Feel sorry for him. And what I did to him."

"Jenna, you can't keep punishing yourself for something that happened years ago," he said softly, his voice filled with compassion. "You did the best you could with the information you had at the time. It's not your fault that new evidence came to light later."

She shook her head, her shoulders slumping as if the burden was too heavy to bear. "But I should have trusted my instincts, Nash. I should have dug deeper, fought harder for the truth. Instead, I just moved on to the next case, and an innocent man lost two years of his life because of me."

"I wish you would have told me all of this. You didn't need to keep it a secret from me."

"I'm just... ashamed of my part in it all. And my responsibility in ruining the man's life."

Nash reached out and gently brushed away a stray tear from her cheek, his fingertips lingering for a moment on her soft skin. "You can't change the past, Jenna, but you can learn from it and use it to make a difference in the future. You have a gift for uncovering the truth, and that's something to be proud of, not ashamed of."

She looked up at him, her eyes searching his for a glimmer of hope. "Do you really believe that?"

He nodded, a small smile tugging at the corners of his mouth. "I do. And I believe in you, Jenna. You're a good person with a kind heart, and you deserve to be happy. Don't let the mistakes of the past rob you of that."

She took a deep, shuddering breath, and he could see the tension slowly easing from her body. "Thank you, Nash. For listening."

"I'm sure what happened is hard to bear. We all often have things we'd like to go back and change. Things we did or didn't do. But... we have to move on with our lives."

"That's what Marly says. That I need to forgive myself. But I don't think I ever will."

"Maybe not, but you do need to learn to live with it and go on living your life."

"I'm sorry I didn't tell you all this from the beginning."

"I knew you were keeping something from me. I could tell." He let out a long sigh. "And that is why I was so angry with you. I just can't have someone lying to me."

"I was trying to protect you."

"I see that now, but all I could see before was you keeping something from me." He looked away for a moment, then back to her. "You see, I dated this woman. Rhonda. We dated a long time. And she kept things from me. Like... like she was seeing someone else."

"I'm sorry." She reached out and touched his arm. "That must have been hard."

He shrugged, a wry smile tugging at his lips. "It was. And it made me wary of anyone who seemed to be hiding something. And she was always spending money. And I was so impressed when you were so intent on staying with your budget. Until… you all of a sudden decided you wanted to tear down the wall, no matter the cost."

"So that's why you were acting so strange about that." She gave him a weak smile. "I just said that I wanted to take out the wall so we'd change the subject. I still don't have the money to spend on it." She shrugged. "And I still like my budgets." She smiled, stronger this time.

He pulled her into his arms, stroking her back, holding her close. He finally pulled back and looked directly into her eyes. "I understand why you kept this from me, but can you promise me one thing? Please don't keep things from me again. Just… tell me. I can't stand secrets and half-truths."

"I won't keep things from you again." She met his gaze. "I promise."

"Good. And to tell the truth, since Milton is my relative, I'm a bit curious now. How about if we look into all of this together?"

"I don't think I should. What if we find out something you don't want to know?"

"I'll take responsibility for that. I'd like to see if we can find out more."

"Are you sure?"

"I'm positive." He nodded and pulled her into his arms again, where she belonged.

She leaned into him. "I've missed you."

He tilted her face up and leaned down and kissed her. "I've missed you too."

As they stood there, holding each other, Nash realized he would do whatever it took to help Jenna find the peace and forgiveness she so desperately needed. Because in that moment, he realized that his feelings for her ran deeper than he had ever imagined possible.

CHAPTER 20

Jenna got up early the next morning, a smile tugging at the corners of her mouth as memories of the previous day flooded her mind. She and Nash were back on good terms. She wasn't sure how she'd gotten so lucky to find a guy like Nash, but she was grateful she had. He seemed to understand her. To get her. He hadn't dismissed her feelings about the events in San Francisco. He had listened, truly listened, but like Marly, he'd encouraged her to move on.

She bounded out of bed and got dressed. The aroma of freshly brewed coffee lured her to the kitchen, where she poured herself a steaming cup. "Hello, liquid motivation," she said, inhaling deeply. "Let's see what kind of trouble we can get into today."

Cup in hand, Jenna stepped out onto the deck. The reflections of the sunrise dyed the clouds a pale pink. The still-cool salty air blew her hair away from her face, stroking her skin.

Yesterday morning she'd been at Beverly's, thinking her world was crumbling around her. And this morning, everything seemed to fall into place like a completed jigsaw puzzle.

"Hey, you."

She turned to see Nash rounding the corner of the house, his smile as bright as the sunrise. Her heart did a little flip as he bounded up the stairs, taking them two at a time.

"Hey, yourself." She grinned back at him, as happiness swept through her at the sight of him. "To what do I owe the pleasure of your company at this early hour?"

His blue eyes sparkled. "Well, I may have inhaled my breakfast just so I could rush over here and…" He leaned in close, his voice dropping to a whisper. "Do this."

He leaned in, capturing her lips in a sweet, lingering kiss. When they finally parted, Jenna felt a bit lightheaded. She recovered and looked up at him. "Was it worth the wait?" she asked, trying to keep her voice steady.

Nash winked, his blue eyes sparkling. "You betcha. I'd skip a thousand breakfasts for that."

She laughed, shaking her head. "You're incorrigible. So, are you here to work on the cottage today?"

"I actually thought that maybe you'd want to come over to my place. There are a ton of boxes in the attic. I haven't been up there in years. It's like every person who ever lived in the house left boxes of stuff up there. We could look through some and see if we come up with anything to help solve the mystery of the letters."

A hint of uncertainty flickered through her. "I guess so."

He took her hands in his. "Are you still wavering on looking at all this? Still worried about what we might find?"

"A little bit."

"I know you're still wrestling with the idea of diving into this mystery. But I promise you, whatever we find, we'll face it together. And who better to have by my side than an expert investigator like yourself?" He grinned, giving her hands a gentle squeeze. "Come on, it'll be an adventure!"

She smiled at his enthusiasm. "Okay, okay. We'll go hunting in your attic."

"Perfect." He wrapped her in a bear hug.

"What was that for?"

"Do I need a reason to hug my best girl?"

"No, probably not." Even searching in a dusty old attic couldn't dampen her mood.

They headed to Nash's and climbed the stairs to the attic. Light flowed in from a large set of windows at the far end. "Where do we start?" The room was packed full of trunks and boxes.

"I've got no clue. I guess we'll just each grab one and get started." He reached out to a shelf, grabbed a box, and handed it to her.

They sat on the floor, sorting through items. Soon, hours had gone by and they hadn't found anything that could have been Milton's. She got up, stretched, and walked over to an old steamer trunk, lifting the lid to peek inside. She knelt beside it and took out an old wedding dress. "Look, Nash. This dress is beautiful. I wonder whose it is?"

Nash glanced over. "I'm not sure. Looks old though."

She carefully set the dress aside. When she reached into the trunk again, she came away with an old family bible. The pages were thin and delicate beneath her fingers as she opened it. "It has the family tree here. Milton is listed. And it looks like he had a sister. Betsy. Oh, they're twins. Look, the same birth date."

Nash got up and came over. "I don't know much about my family many generations back." After a quick scan of the family tree, he turned the trunk and reached in. The old leather book he pulled out had a rusted metal lock, which popped open easily when he tested it. "Guess that lock didn't keep this very secure."

He handed it to her. She opened it slowly. "Oh, look. It's Betsy's."

"Maybe it might have some clues. At least it's from the right time period. Why don't you look at it and I'll search more boxes. Surely old Milton has a box in here somewhere."

"You sure you want me to read this?"

He touched her face lightly. "I'm sure."

She sat down and began to pore over the pages. Soon she was lost in the everyday details of life in the 1920s. The weather, who was dating whom, and even mentions of a few town festivals.

A short while later, Nash interrupted her reading. "Bingo. Found something. It even has his name written on the box." Nash carried the box over and took off the lid. "Look, here's a photo right on top." He flipped it over. "It says Vera and Milton on the back. They look young." He narrowed his eyes. "Doesn't this woman look like the one from your photograph?"

She reached out for it and examined it closely. "It does." She frowned. "Why does the name Vera sound familiar?"

"Not sure." He reached in and pulled out some old leather books. "Looks like these might have been his logs when he was the lighthouse keeper. Ships coming in and leaving. Storms and how bad they were."

She turned back to the journal, eager to find out more. "Oh, here's Vera's name right in Betsy's journal. Looks like Milton and Vera were friends. Oh, maybe more than friends. Betsy says that Milton was sweet on Vera."

"But then why would he have been the go-between for some other man writing to Vera? Assuming those letters were to Vera."

"I don't know."

Nash reached down a hand. "I think we've

done enough digging around for the day. Let's take a break. I actually have to go out to a job site for a bit."

She took his hand, and he pulled her to her feet. "I think I'll go back to my cottage. Do you mind if I take the journal with me?"

"No, sure. Take it. I'll drop you off on my way."

"I think I'll walk. Wouldn't mind some fresh air after all this dust."

They headed downstairs, and he walked her to the door. "Dinner tonight?"

"I'd like that." She left and headed back to her cottage, but at the last minute turned and decided to stop by Second Finds to see Dale. Maybe he had found out something, even though she'd told him she was dropping the whole thing.

She walked into Second Finds, and Dale greeted her warmly. "Jenna, there you are. I was just getting ready to call you. I found out something. Not sure if it will help, but at least it's something."

"What did you find out?"

"I did some digging in the deed records for your cottage. Your cottage used to be owned by the Whitmores. Vera Whitmore's father bought it for her."

"Vera?" Her heart thudded in her chest and her pulse raced.

"Yes. The Whitmores have been on the island almost since the day it was discovered. They're Miss Eleanor's family."

"She's a Whitmore?"

"Born a Whitmore. Married a Griffin, but most people in town still think of her as a Whitmore. The Carlisles used to live next door to the Whitmores at one time. Then the Carlisles built a new house further out on the point. They're among the oldest families that settled the island."

"Thank you for that, Dale." She started to tell him about what she and Nash had found, but decided she better not without talking to Nash. After all, it was his family member who might have been in love with Vera.

"And, funny thing." Dale shook his head. "That necklace Tori found in the theater. It was Vera's necklace. She's sure popping up in strange places these days."

That's where she'd heard the name. Beverly had told her about the pendant and that it was Vera's.

"That is strange how her name keeps coming up."

"You could ask Miss Eleanor about Vera. See if she knows anything," Dale suggested.

"Maybe." But Miss Eleanor had already said that some secrets are best kept in the past. "I should go, but thanks for your help."

She hurried home, poured herself a large glass of iced tea, and settled down with the journal. Soon she was lost in the pages. Betsy wrote a lot about her brother. It was obvious the two of them were close. Toward the back of the journal, she found a letter tucked between the pages. On the page next to the letter, Betsy had written again about her brother. As she read the words, her heart caught in her chest. Betsy was supposed to deliver this letter to Vera. A letter where Milton told Vera how he felt about her. But Betsy had seen Vera kissing another man. Some guy named Lawrence. It looked like Vera never got his letter if Betsy still had it in her journal.

Poor Milton and his unrequited love. But it seemed like Milton cared more about Vera's happiness than his own. He'd agreed to deliver letters to her so no one would find out.

She continued reading the journal and

smiled as Betsy fell in love and got married. Had two kids. She even mentioned that Milton had left his job as the lighthouse keeper and how mad she was at the town. And Milton for not just telling the town the truth about the letters. But Milton had remained true to Vera, never revealing her secret.

But as she finished reading the journal, she still had no idea who Lawrence was.

CHAPTER 21

J enna flung open the door when Nash arrived and tugged on his hand, pulling him inside. "You'll never guess what I found out. I have so much to tell you."

He chuckled. "Okay, tell me what you learned."

"Milton was in love with Vera Whitmore."

Nash's brows shot up. "Whitmore? As in *the* Whitmores?"

"Yes, like Miss Eleanor." She nodded vigorously. "And he wrote Vera a letter professing his love, but when his sister went to deliver it, she found Vera in the arms of another man. Some Lawrence guy."

"Wow, that's some story."

Jenna continued, her words tumbling out in

a rush. "From what I've gathered, Betsy, Milton, and Vera grew up together. They were the best of friends, inseparable since childhood. But as time passed, Milton's feelings for Vera deepened into something more. He fell head over heels in love with her."

"Milton and Vera?"

"Yes, exactly. But in the end, Milton only wanted Vera to be happy, even if it meant sacrificing his own heart. He never found the courage to tell her how much he truly cared for her. Instead, he agreed to deliver the letters from Lawrence, keeping their secret safe."

"We have no idea who this Lawrence guy is?"

"None."

"So we only know part of the story." He scanned her face. "And do you want to dig around more and find out who he is?"

She paused, considering the question. The mystery of Lawrence's identity tugged at her curiosity, but a deeper part of her knew that some secrets were meant to remain hidden. "No, I don't think I do. Vera, Lawrence, *and* Milton must have had a good reason to keep this all a secret. I think we should do just like Milton did, and keep Vera's secret."

"You sure?" His blue eyes searched her face, as if looking for any hint of doubt.

"I am sure. Like Miss Eleanor said. Some things are just better kept buried in the past."

"I'm good with keeping it a secret if you are." He took her hands and squeezed them.

"I am. If I've learned nothing else from my investigative reporter career, it's when to admit a story doesn't need to be told. I think we should just let all three of these people rest in peace, secure in their secrets." A sense of peace washed over her, knowing they were doing the right thing.

"Then that's what we'll do," Nash agreed, his voice soft and supportive. He pulled her closer, wrapping his arms around her in a comforting embrace. Jenna leaned into him, feeling the warmth of his body and the steadiness of his presence.

She finally pulled back slightly and looked up at him. "Oh, and that dress we found was Betsy's. There was a wedding photo in the journal too. She was wearing that dress."

"So much history up in that old attic, isn't there?" He paused and frowned. "So, do you think we should go and see Miss Eleanor? Tell her what we've found?"

"I was just thinking the same thing. It involves her family as much as yours. And I'll give her the photo of her great-aunt. She should have that."

Nash glanced at his watch. "If we hurry, we can catch Miss Eleanor when she's out walking her dog, Winston. She walks him every afternoon. You can set your watch by it."

"Great, let's go."

They hurried over to the street near Miss Eleanor's house, and sure enough, at about four twenty Miss Eleanor appeared homeward bound with her cavalier pup, Winston, trotting at her side. They stood at the gate to her front walkway, waiting for her.

Miss Eleanor gave them both an appraising glance as she walked up to them. Winston wagged his tail in an enthusiastic greeting. Miss Eleanor's expression remained neutral as she spoke. "I assume you want to see me?"

"We do, Miss Eleanor. Something we'd like to talk to you about." Jenna bent down and petted the dog, who promptly licked her face, and she laughed as she stood back up.

"Well, you best come inside. No use keeping Winston out here in the heat any longer." She bustled through the gate, her movements efficient and purposeful. Pausing, she turned back toward Jenna and Nash, an expectant look on her face. "You coming? I haven't got all day, you know."

Jenna followed Nash and Miss Eleanor into the stately house, taking in the meticulously decorated foyer with its polished hardwood floors and elegant wall sconces. As they stepped into the formal living room on the left, Jenna's eyes were drawn to the large, gilded frames housing paintings of serene landscapes and the delicate floral print upholstery adorning the plush couches.

Sunlight struggled to penetrate the heavy drapes flanking the tall windows, casting the room in a soft, muted glow. A magnificent bookshelf dominated the far wall, its shelves lined with leather-bound volumes and family photographs.

"Come in. Sit. I'll bring us some lemonade." Her words were more a command than a request.

Miss Eleanor returned, carefully balancing a tray of three large glasses of lemonade, and handed each of them one. She settled herself on an armchair that practically shouted its history with its intricately carved fretwork on the armrest and embroidered seat.

Miss Eleanor took a sip of her lemonade, the ice clinking gently against the glass as she fixed her gaze on them. "Now, what did you want to talk to me about?"

Nash looked at Jenna. She took a deep breath, her heart pounding as she prepared to broach the delicate subject. "We wanted to talk to you about... Vera. Vera Whitmore."

Miss Eleanor quickly hid her surprise, but not before Jenna caught the tiniest bit of fear in her eyes. "My great-aunt. What do you want to know? She left the island a long time ago and never returned."

"The letters I found in my cottage. I believe they were Vera's."

Miss Eleanor let out a soft sigh. "I was afraid they were. She lived in your cottage for a while. She was in her twenties and early thirties, I'd guess. It was considered being a spinster if you were single at that age back then, you know."

"I think the letters were from a man named Lawrence."

Miss Eleanor gave her a hard stare. "You think that why?"

"It's a pretty long story, but Milton Carlisle

—Nash's some-number-of-greats uncle—grew up with Vera. He and his twin sister, Betsy. They were all friends. And I guess Milton realized he had feelings for Vera."

Miss Eleanor's forehead crinkled. "He did?" She shook her head as one stray beam of sunlight managed to fight its way through the drapes and highlight her silvery hair. "Never heard that."

"He did. But before Milton could tell Vera how he felt, Betsy found Vera with this Lawrence guy."

The older woman raised an eyebrow. "She did?"

"She told Milton, but Milton said they should keep it a secret."

The room fell silent as Miss Eleanor digested the information, absently tapping her fingers on the armrest of her chair. She finally looked over, her brow creased. "How did you find all this out?"

"I… I read it in Betsy's journal." Jenna blushed slightly, waiting for the stern reprimand she knew was coming.

But the older woman just paused and said, "I see."

Recovering from her surprise, she rushed to

explain, "I read it because we were hoping to find out what happened to everyone. They all feel so real to me now." She dug in her tote, pulled out the photo, and held it out. "Anyway, I thought you'd like to have this photo of Vera, and who I assume is Lawrence."

Miss Eleanor took it, her eyes carefully studying the photo. She ran a finger over the print before looking up. "I don't have many photos of her. She left the island, and I was told my grandfather—Vera's own brother—took down all the pictures of her."

"Do you know why she left?" Jenna asked softly.

"No, I don't. I'm sure she had her reasons. The same reasons she kept these letters a secret." Eleanor looked up and stared at both of them with a hard look. "And what are you going to do with all this information?"

She looked at Nash, and he nodded. "We're… we're not going to do anything with it. Their story isn't ours to tell." She reached into her tote once more and took out the wooden box that had been hidden in the floorboards of her cottage. "And these are yours too. Vera's letters."

Eleanor took the box and set it on her lap,

her fingers tracing the intricate design on the top. "Thank you," she said softly. "Vera must have had her reason for keeping this a secret. I appreciate you respecting that." The older woman looked out toward the window. "Some secrets are best kept hidden, aren't they?"

Jenna was certain Miss Eleanor was talking more about herself than Vera. Eleanor finally looked up at them, coming out of her thoughts. "I appreciate you figuring out these were Vera's and returning them to me. You're quite the investigator."

"Thank you. I'm just glad I could return them to you."

Miss Eleanor smiled. "Now, would you like more lemonade?"

"We should go. I just wanted you to have the letters and the photo. To hear what we found out." She and Nash stood. "Thank you for seeing us."

Miss Eleanor rose. "Thank you for bringing these to me. And... for your discretion." She walked them to the door. As they walked down the steps, Miss Eleanor called out, "Jenna?"

She turned around.

"Welcome to the island. And... you're a great addition to our little community. If you ever need anything, just ask." With that, the woman turned and slipped inside her house, the door closing softly behind her.

Nash nudged her gently with his elbow. "That's a big compliment coming from Miss Eleanor. She's not very free with them."

"I'm just glad the letters and photo went back to where they belong."

"And you're okay with just letting this story die? Never finding out who Lawrence was or what happened to Vera?"

"Absolutely. Your uncle went to great lengths to protect Vera and her secrets. Secrets that involve your family and Miss Eleanor. Milton even lost his job because of it. I think it's the least we can do to respect his wishes."

He brushed a lock of hair away from her face, his fingers grazing her cheek. "You, Jenna, are a very kindhearted woman."

A warmth spread through her at his words. "You're not so bad yourself," she said, trying to keep her voice light as her emotions raced wild.

His expression grew serious. "When I thought things were ruined between us, I... I just didn't know what I was going to do. I know we haven't known each other for that long, but I do care about you. Very much." He trailed a finger along her cheekbone, leaving a trail of tingling sensation. "How would you feel about me kissing you right now? Right out here on the street where anyone could see."

Her heart fluttered. "I can't see that it would be a problem." She turned her face up to him in invitation.

He captured her lips in a tender, lingering kiss that made her forget the world around them. The sound of a car horn honking caused them to break apart, and Nash glanced up, a grin spreading across his face. "Pretty sure the whole town just found out about us. That was the Jenkins twins from over in Moonbeam Bay. They come here quite often. And they're known for being the biggest spreaders of gossip in both towns—maybe in the whole state."

"And how do you feel about everyone knowing about us?"

"I couldn't be happier. I want to shout it out loud."

"That would be fine with me."

He opened his mouth wide, and she laughed, placing her hand over his mouth. "Maybe not right outside Miss Eleanor's."

CHAPTER 22

Jenna hurried to Coastal Coffee the next morning, hoping to catch Nash before he left. Beverly greeted her warmly with a friendly embrace. "Good morning. You just missed Nash. But I heard the news."

She frowned slightly. Hadn't she and Nash just agreed to keep Vera's secret?

"He said you two had worked out your differences and are seeing each other again." Beverly's face lit up with a wide, genuine smile.

"Oh, that." She grinned. "There is that bit of news."

"And I ran into the Jenkins twins, who told me they caught Nash kissing you out in front of Miss Eleanor's." Beverly laughed. "Those two find out everything first. But I'm happy for the two of you."

Jenna felt a blush creep across her face.

Beverly took her hand. "Come join Dorothy and Tori. Have you met Dorothy yet? She owns Bayside Bed and Breakfast."

"No, I haven't. But I don't want to intrude on their breakfast."

"Don't be silly," Beverly insisted as she led her over to her table.

"Jenna, please join us," Tori insisted with a welcoming smile.

"Dorothy, this is Jenna."

"Great to meet you, Jenna. I've heard so much about you."

"You have?" Jenna took Dorothy's outstretched hand.

"Of course. And I heard you're fixing up the old Weston place."

"There's not much left to do. It's beginning to look just like I imagined." She laughed. "Well, except for the couches I inherited. I'm afraid they need to be recovered, but I'm not much of a sewing expert. Last time I touched a sewing machine was home economics in high school."

"You're in luck then, because I am an

expert. I could help you make them," Dorothy offered, her eyes lighting up at the prospect.

"Dorothy here is our crafty expert. Sewing. Knitting. Anything crafty," Beverly added, her voice full of admiration. "She's got magic in her fingers, I swear."

"If you're serious, I'd love to. Even though I did need help with some of the repairs on the cottage, I do enjoy fixing things up myself. There's something so satisfying about breathing new life into old things."

"Perfect. I'd love to teach you. We'll make plans to go to the mainland and pick out fabric." Dorothy's eyes shone with enthusiasm.

"You know, I have an overstuffed chair that I'd love to recover. Mind if I join in on the lessons?" Tori asked, leaning forward with interest.

"Sure, that would be wonderful," Dorothy said, then motioned to the empty chair beside her. "Sit and join us, Jenna. Please."

Jenna sat down at the table and soon was embraced as one of their own. She felt a warmth and acceptance that had escaped her for so long. It was a simple meal with friends, but it felt like so much more. She wasn't sure how she'd gone from feeling like an outsider in

Magnolia Key to feeling like she belonged, but happiness crept through her as they sat, chatted, and made plans.

As she was about to leave the cafe, Beverly caught her arm gently. "So, looks like you're becoming one of us. I knew you'd fit right in."

"I'm starting to feel like it."

Beverly gave her a smile, her eyes twinkling with warmth. "You are one, a real local now. Welcome home, Jenna."

Jenna saw Nash almost every day over the next few weeks. He worked on the cottage and they took long walks on the beach, talking about their lives, getting to know each other better. She met his family—all of them—and that was quite an ordeal. She'd been so nervous to meet them, but they'd all been lovely to her.

Now Nash stood in her kitchen, fixing the last window that needed adjusting. "There you have it. I think that's all of them."

"Thank you. I was using a ruler to prop it open."

"Can't have your contractor leaving jobs unfinished, now can we?" He walked over and pulled her into his arms. "Like, I think I left that last kiss unfinished."

"Oh, is kissing part of the services you provide as a contractor?" She grinned up at him.

"Only for my special clients." He winked and settled his lips on hers.

When they parted, his arms still encircled her waist. "And I've been wanting to talk to you."

Before she could respond, a knock echoed through the cottage. "Hold that thought, I've got to get that."

"Someone has lousy timing," he grumbled good-naturedly before stealing a quick kiss and reluctantly releasing her.

She hurried to the front door and threw it open. Her eyes widened in surprise. "Marly. What are you doing here? You're not supposed to be here until Friday."

Marly laughed, her eyes shining with excitement. "I thought I'd come surprise you early. Hope that's okay. I've missed you."

"Of course it is." She hugged her sister tightly, realizing how much she'd missed seeing her all the time. "I've missed you, too."

As they stepped inside, Marly's eyes darted

around the place. "And I couldn't wait to see... your place."

Jenna grinned at her sister. "You mean meet Nash?"

"Did I hear my name?" Nash came walking out of the kitchen.

"Nash, this is my sister, Marly. She's early. You'll soon find out Marly is full of surprises."

He reached out his hand. "Marly, so great to meet you."

Marly gave him an obvious once over. "Good to meet you too. The guy that finally got my sis to move on with her life."

"Marly..." she warned.

Her sister grinned, clearly enjoying the moment. "Just teasing. Kinda."

Nash took the teasing in stride. "Hey, I've got to head to Mom's. You'll still be over this evening?"

Jenna hesitated, glancing at her sister. She didn't want Marly to feel left out or like she was infringing on their plans. "Marly? You up for it? I'm supposed to have dinner with his family tonight."

To her relief, Marly waved off her concerns. "But I don't want to intrude," she said, though

Jenna could tell she was intrigued by the idea of meeting Nash's family."

"You won't be. Mom believes in the more the merrier. And I'm warning you, there's a lot of us. And we're noisy." Nash brushed a kiss on Jenna's cheek and walked toward the door. "We'll see you two for dinner." He gave her one last smile before slipping outside.

She turned to Marly, a wide smile spreading across her face. "Well, looks like you're getting the full Magnolia Key experience. Dinner with the Carlisles."

"Hey, I can't wait to meet them all. And I'm so glad to see you've got that sparkle back in your eyes." Marly glanced around the cottage. "So... tell me everything. Looks like the cottage is finished."

"It is."

"And you and Nash?"

"Couldn't be better." She couldn't help the immediate smile that swept across her lips.

Marly reached out and took her hand. "I'm so glad to see you so happy. You deserve it."

"I've finally found a way to make peace with my past. To move on. I'll always regret my part in it all, but... I can't change what happened.

I've just given myself a little grace and forgiveness."

"I'm proud of you, sis."

"Hope you'll still be talking to me after dinner. Nash wasn't kidding when he said his family was... a lot." She laughed and linked her arm through her sister's, leading her further into the cottage. "Come on, I'll give you the grand tour. And then we can catch up before we head over to the Carlisles'."

They went to the Carlisles' that evening and Marly and Pam hit it off immediately. They dove into an animated conversation, their laughter carrying across the backyard. It warmed her heart to see her sister getting along so well with Nash's family—even when it involved her and Pam dissecting Nash and Jenna's relationship in enthusiastic detail. Jenna just shook her head and let them have at it, knowing it was futile to protest.

Nash appeared at her side and handed her a cold beer. "You doing okay?"

She smiled, feeling a surge of contentment wash over her. "I've never been better," she assured him, meaning every word.

Nash nodded, but there was a flicker of hesitation in his expression. "There's something

I've been wanting to tell you," he began, his voice low and serious.

"Oh, right. When Marly interrupted us earlier, you were starting to say something."

"Yeah, I was." Nash took a deep breath, his gaze intense. "I know this might not be the best time, but I need to tell you, anyway. It can't wait any longer."

A trickle of apprehension ran down Jenna's spine as she studied his face, trying to prepare herself for whatever he was about to say. "What is it?" she asked softly, her heart beginning to race.

Nash reached out and took her hand in his, his calloused fingers entwining with hers. "I wanted to tell you..." He paused, his eyes locking with hers. "That I love you, Jenna."

Her breath caught in her throat and she could only stare at him, her mind reeling as she tried to process what he said. Her heart soared as his words sank in. She marveled at the depth of emotion in his eyes, feeling as if she might burst with happiness. "You... you love me?" she managed to whisper, her voice trembling.

"I do. I'm madly, deeply, hopelessly in love with you. And I wouldn't have it any other way," he said, his voice husky with emotion.

Overcome with joy, she threw her arms around his neck, pulling him close. She breathed in his familiar scent, feeling his heart beat in rhythm with hers. "Oh, Nash. I love you too. So much," she whispered against his ear.

Their moment was interrupted as Nash's nephews came racing up to him. "Uncle Nash, you gonna kiss Miss Jenna all night, or you gonna play catch with us?" the older boy asked.

Nash's laugh rang out across the backyard, warm and rich. "Now, that's a tough choice, guys. A tough choice."

"Boys, leave your uncle alone," Pam called out from where she and Marly stood grinning.

Nash turned back to her, his eyes twinkling. "Now, where were we?"

Jenna bit her lip, trying to suppress a grin, but it was impossible as pure happiness surged through her. "You were about to kiss me again and tell me you love me again," she teased.

"Ah, yes. That." He reached out and cupped her face with his strong hand. "I love you, Jenna. Very much. You've been such an unexpected surprise in my life. You have my whole heart."

And her heart somersaulted in her chest at

his words. "I love you, Nash Carlisle. For being so understanding, so patient, and…" She grinned mischievously at him. "For being a good kisser."

He laughed out loud, then leaned in and kissed her again, his lips soft and warm against hers. Jenna melted into the kiss, feeling truly at home for the first time in a very long time.

"Oh, and another thing," Nash said as he pulled back slightly and looked down at her. "I was thinking we'd start on taking down that wall between the kitchen and the living room."

"But I told you, I don't have the funds for that."

"That's the good thing about having me as your boyfriend. You'll get free labor and I'll salvage up the other supplies. Won't cost you a penny."

"Nash, that's incredibly generous of you," she said, her voice soft with emotion. "But I don't want you to feel obligated to take on more work on my behalf. You've already done so much…"

He grinned down at her, his blue eyes crinkling at the corners. "It's not an obligation, Jenna. I *want* to do this for you."

"Then thank you. It will look great once that

wall is gone. It will really open up the space and bring in more light."

"And if it makes you happy, it makes me happy." He slipped his arm around her waist again and they stood in the shade of the live oak in the corner of his parents' backyard.

Standing there with him, surrounded by the warmth and easy acceptance of his family, a profound sense of belonging washed over her. In just a few short months, Magnolia Key had worked its way into her heart, offering her a safe haven from her troubled past and a chance to build a new life. The island's unhurried pace, charming ambiance, and welcoming community had woven its magic around her and finally brought her the peace she needed.

CHAPTER 23

Eleanor sat out on her porch, the evening sky stretching out before her like a vast canvas painted in an inky dark blue, broken only by the sparkling stars and the faint glow of a crescent moon. Winston snored peacefully at her feet, his gentle breaths providing a soothing rhythm to the quiet night. The salt-tinged breeze carried the distant whisper of waves lapping against the shore, a constant reminder of the island's embrace.

She rocked slowly back and forth in her well-worn chair, the creaking of the wood a familiar sound that had accompanied countless evenings spent in this very spot. How many nights had she sat out here on her porch, gazing at the stars and pondering life's mysteries? In the very same house she grew up in, where the walls held a lifetime of memories, both joyous and painful. Each creak of the chair seemed to echo with whispers of the past, a nudge reminding her of the years that had slipped by like grains of sand through her fingers. She could almost hear the sounds from summers long past, feel the warmth of her momma's embrace, and smell the scent of her daddy's pipe tobacco lingering in the air.

These walls held so many secrets. Secrets that had been carefully guarded, hidden away from prying eyes and curious minds. She herself had kept secrets, buried deep within her heart. Sometimes, she knew, one had to do that—keep a secret to protect themselves. Is that what Vera had done? Had she had some secret affair with someone that the family knew nothing about? Or maybe the family did know, and that knowledge had driven a wedge between them, leading to Vera's eventual departure from the island.

Eleanor didn't know, and she suspected she'd probably never find out. She just hoped Vera had found her happiness, found peace. That her great-aunt had chased after what she wanted most in life, even if it meant leaving everything familiar behind.

But life had its mysteries, and some were meant to remain unsolved, floating like distant stars in the infinite expanse of the night sky.

Vera had been a stronger woman than she was. Because she, herself, hadn't been strong enough to stand up to her father all those years ago. She hadn't had the courage to defy his wishes. And look what had happened. She'd lost her chance at a life filled with passion and joy.

Instead, she'd married Theodore Griffin just like her daddy had wanted her to do. Theodore. Never Teddy or Ted. He was a man who demanded formality, even in the most intimate of settings.

She should probably say she missed Theodore now that he was gone, but, to tell the truth, she didn't much. She guessed that's what happened when you married someone you weren't in love with, when you settled for a comfortable life of stability rather than trusting your heart and standing up for what you really wanted.

She closed her eyes against the memories, letting the gentle breeze brush against her face, remembering a wish of her own she'd made all those years ago. A dream she'd long abandoned.

The stars twinkled above as if each one was someone's wish, a secret desire whispered into the darkness. A wish that might come true, if one only had the strength to believe in it.

I hope you enjoyed this book in the Magnolia Key series. And, there's more to Eleanor's story, of course. We'll find out more in the next book, *Bayside Beginnings*. In the next book, Darlene—the owner of Bayside B&B—invites her granddaughter, Felicity, to come stay for the summer. Felicity is burned out from her teaching job and needing a break. But she finds much more than that…

And Eleanor? Let's just say she gets a big surprise in the next book when more secrets are revealed. Oh, and more of Vera's secrets come out too. Lots going on in this series!

As always, I appreciate your support and hope you're enjoying a little escape into my books.

ALSO BY KAY CORRELL

COMFORT CROSSING ~ THE SERIES

The Shop on Main - Book One

The Memory Box - Book Two

The Christmas Cottage - A Holiday Novella (Book 2.5)

The Letter - Book Three

The Christmas Scarf - A Holiday Novella (Book 3.5)

The Magnolia Cafe - Book Four

The Unexpected Wedding - Book Five

The Wedding in the Grove (crossover short story between series - Josephine and Paul from The Letter.)

LIGHTHOUSE POINT ~ THE SERIES

Wish Upon a Shell - Book One

Wedding on the Beach - Book Two

Love at the Lighthouse - Book Three

Cottage near the Point - Book Four

Return to the Island - Book Five

Bungalow by the Bay - Book Six

Christmas Comes to Lighthouse Point - Book Seven

CHARMING INN ~ Return to Lighthouse Point

One Simple Wish - Book One

Two of a Kind - Book Two

Three Little Things - Book Three

Four Short Weeks - Book Four

Five Years or So - Book Five

Six Hours Away - Book Six

Charming Christmas - Book Seven

SWEET RIVER ~ THE SERIES

A Dream to Believe in - Book One

A Memory to Cherish - Book Two

A Song to Remember - Book Three

A Time to Forgive - Book Four

A Summer of Secrets - Book Five

A Moment in the Moonlight - Book Six

MOONBEAM BAY ~ THE SERIES

The Parker Women - Book One

The Parker Cafe - Book Two

A Heather Parker Original - Book Three

The Parker Family Secret - Book Four

Grace Parker's Peach Pie - Book Five

The Perks of Being a Parker - Book Six

BLUE HERON COTTAGES ~ THE SERIES

Memories of the Beach - Book One

Walks along the Shore - Book Two

Bookshop near the Coast - Book Three

Restaurant on the Wharf - Book Four

Lilacs by the Sea - Book Five

Flower Shop on Magnolia - Book Six

Christmas by the Bay - Book Seven

Sea Glass from the Past - Book Eight

MAGNOLIA KEY ~ THE SERIES

Saltwater Sunrise - Book One

Encore Echoes - Book Two

Coastal Candlelight - Book Three

Tidal Treasures - Book Four

Bayside Beginnings - Book Five

And more to come!

CHRISTMAS SEASHELLS AND SNOWFLAKES

Seaside Christmas Wishes

WIND CHIME BEACH ~ A stand-alone novel

INDIGO BAY ~

Sweet Days by the Bay - Kay's complete collection of stories in the Indigo Bay series

ABOUT THE AUTHOR

Kay Correll is a USA Today bestselling author of sweet, heartwarming stories that are a cross between women's fiction and contemporary romance. She is known for her charming small towns, quirky townsfolk, and the enduring strong friendships between the women in her books.

Kay splits her time between the southwest coast of Florida and the Midwest of the U.S. and can often be found out and about with her camera, taking a myriad of photographs, often incorporating them into her book covers. When not lost in her writing or photography, she can be found spending time with her ever-supportive husband, knitting, or playing with her puppies - a cavalier who is too cute for his own good and a naughty but adorable Australian shepherd. Their five boys are all grown now and while she misses the rowdy boy-noise chaos, she is thoroughly enjoying her empty nest years.

Learn more about Kay and her books at kaycorrell.com

While you're there, sign up for her newsletter to hear about new releases, sales, and giveaways.

WHERE TO FIND ME:
My shop: shop.kaycorrell.com
My author website: kaycorrell.com
authorcontact@kaycorrell.com

Join my Facebook Reader Group. We have lots of fun and you'll hear about sales and new releases first!
www.facebook.com/groups/KayCorrell/

I love to hear from my readers. Feel free to contact me at authorcontact@kaycorrell.com

facebook.com/KayCorrellAuthor

instagram.com/kaycorrell

pinterest.com/kaycorrellauthor

amazon.com/author/kaycorrell

bookbub.com/authors/kay-correll